The Matriarch

The Matriarch

Linda Lysakowski

ISBN 978-1-257-80470-2

Dedication

This book is dedicated to the many guides I've had in my spiritual journey, especially Sister Joy, who is now touching God.

Contents

PART I

PART II

PART I

Chapter 1

New York

Ever since she was a young girl, three things fascinated Leslie Castle Flynn—mountains, trees and cowboys. At the early age of twelve, she knew that these three things would somehow, someday come together to change her life.

Now, more than forty years later, as the plane left JFK International Airport on that humid June evening, heading for Rome to meet George, she mused about how it all began. Her brother George, now Cardinal Castle, had always thought she was too much like their father, who had been a dreamer, never accomplishing anything in life, but always clinging to those crazy dreams. Leslie recalled the first evening she and George had talked about her "mountaintop experience." He had first thought it was another one of Leslie's crazy dreams, but as their two-hour conversation unfolded, George recognized that Leslie was dead serious this time and that her experience would drastically change Leslie's life and his own, as well as the lives of countless other people.

George had his mother Greta's personality, down to earth, rock solid, as her German heritage dictated. Leslie, on the other hand, remembered being chided by her mother for building "castles in the air," and she knew that Greta sometimes cursed Henry Castle for passing along those idle genes to her only daughter. Greta Castle, whose parents had emigrated from Germany, brought to the marriage with Henry Castle a handsome dowry and a proclivity for practicality. Henry was attracted to Greta by her tidy appearance, her air of authority, and of course, the dowry that would help finance his dreams.

Although the Castle family was never destitute, Henry's dream of a life of luxury never came to pass. But he always made sure there was food on the table and Greta's frugal nature saved the family from the embarrassment of having bill collectors at the door. Unlike some of their neighbors, they never bought anything "on tick" but paid cash for the few luxuries they had. Greta could stretch a dollar like few women in their neighborhood; she shopped at thrift stores, grew her own vegetables, and sewed most of the family's clothing.

In some ways, Leslie's life was not all that much different from her father's. Although she had a master's degree in business, with a minor in psychology, she was always working just long enough and hard enough to finance the big dream. Like her father, Leslie married a practical, consistent person who kept her grounded. Leslie and Michael had a seamless marriage for almost twenty-seven years and had three beautiful children before that fateful day when Michael had a sudden heart attack while driving on the New York State Throughway and crashed head on into a tractor-trailer.

Days of numbness followed, with only friends, family, and faith holding together the fragile pieces of her life. Leslie thanked God every day for her brother George—then Bishop of the Diocese of Metuchen, New Jersey—for his calm ability to see her through this tragedy of Michael's death just as he had seven years earlier when their parents had died within two weeks of each other.

Once the shock of Michael's death passed, Leslie had to face the reality that she was now alone. She and Michael had been a couple for so long, it was hard to imagine life without him. Certainly her children were a consolation and each of them in their own way carried Michael within them. Valerie was the most like her father, the practical one, the engineer, the one who would always know the right thing to do. Alex had Michael's good looks and intelligence and was a little bit of a dreamer like Leslie, but he always tempered his dreams with reality, and at times sounded so much like Michael that it scared Leslie. And then, there was their youngest progeny, Andre, whose sensitive nature and deep faith could only have come from Michael. True, George's influence on Andre was evident in the fact that Andre was heading off to the seminary to become a priest, but it was Michael's influence and deep spirituality that Leslie credited with this decision; although she would never tell George that she thought Michael Flynn had always been a better Catholic than anyone in the Castle family, even George.

The touch of the flight attendant on her arm roused Leslie from her reverie. As the handsome, blue-eyed young man offered a glass of wine before takeoff, Leslie said a silent prayer of thanks for the power and wealth of the Catholic Church. George had arranged a first class seat for her trip to the Vatican. Leslie was never able to sleep on planes, and now, despite the plush leather sets, the Enya tape on the new iPod Valerie had given her for her fifty-fifth birthday, the solicitous flight attendant, and the glass of cabernet sauvignon he would have at her side in a minute, she knew she would certainly not sleep on this flight. Leslie was not much of a drinker; she rarely even had a glass of wine because of the calories and the artificial preservatives. But tonight was an exception. She would even splurge and accept the Godiva chocolate offered by the flight attendant, throwing all caution to the wind, not to mention the possibility of not fitting into the size five slacks she was proud of wearing after three children and menopause. She needed all the comfort she could get tonight. She had already endured six hours in the air flying from Reno to New York, preceded by a forty-minute drive to the Reno airport from her home in the Carson Valley. The eight-and-a-half-hour flight from New York to Rome, combined with a nine-hour time difference would leave her totally wiped out when she landed in Rome, but she was too tense, too excited to even think of sleeping. George would have a limousine waiting for her, scheduled to whisk her off to her plush suite in the Vatican Hotel. There she would theoretically catch up on her sleep beneath the soft white eiderdown comforter she knew would be waiting in the dimly lit, quiet room. She should be rested for her dinner with George tomorrow evening. But sleep would be an elusive concept for Leslie this evening.

Sipping her wine, settling the earphones comfortably on her head, kicking off her Aigner loafers, and stretching out in the luxurious leather reclining seat, Leslie's mind was drawn back to her girlhood. She and George were arguing about their favorite colors. He was convinced that green was the best color of them all, "after all, look at all the green God put on this earth," he would say. Leslie, perhaps just to be contrary, had always claimed red was her favorite and needed no further reason than that it was the color of strawberries and red licorice. Of course, any good psychologist would tell them that Leslie preferred red because she was the more aggressive and George's peaceful, gentle soul would be more aligned with green. But to a twelve- and fourteen-year-old, the color of grass and trees versus red licorice seemed consequential enough to stir up hours of sibling squabbles.

Despite the fact that she preferred red to George's favorite green, Leslie had always been drawn to trees. She climbed trees at every opportunity; she drew trees when she doodled; and she always lined her walls with photographs or paintings of trees everywhere she lived. When she and Michael moved to West Hartford, she was pleased to find a home on a quiet, tree-lined street, providing her with trees to admire, to tend, and for the children (and maybe even Leslie herself) to climb. She filled the Flynn home with her collection of bonsai trees and photographs she had taken of all sorts of trees. Above their fireplace stood her pride and joy—the rendering of her favorite willow tree that her best friend Sara had painted for Michael and her as a wedding gift. Leslie and Sara had spent many hours picnicking under that willow tree, where they shared their first cigarette when they were twelve, and where they shared a kiss with their first boyfriends. Although the willow tree was special for them, it was usually not the lush green trees that attracted Leslie. She much preferred the naked winter trees, or the brightly hued fall foliage; the more twisted and turned the trunks were, the better.

Then there was the tree she always stopped to touch on her walk home from school. It was a solid oak with a gnarled trunk that had an odd growth on it resembling a woman's behind. She never knew why that tree fascinated her so much, but she knew it was intriguing enough to make her stop beneath it and spend a minute embracing its bark every day on the walk home from St. Monica's. Leslie thought about that tree for a long time and wondered if it still stood on Maple Street. She always thought it odd that the street was named Maple but was populated by dozens, if not hundreds, of oak trees. Well, such was life; sometimes things went by one name and Leslie often thought they should have another, especially people; although, truth be told, people fascinated her just slightly more than trees.

Still caught in her tree fantasy, Leslie thought again about her best childhood friend, Sara, and their numerous tree-climbing adventures. Apple trees, oak trees, sycamores, it didn't really matter, but they both seemed to love climbing trees. Maybe it was because they both had older brothers they constantly tagged after and were considered the neighborhood's tomboys.

The business man seated next to her gave a start when Leslie laughed out loud, remembering the time she had lost her shoe climbing a huge felled tree up on Stone Mountain. Try as she and Sara might, they never did find that shoe. And Leslie had to hobble home on one shoe, trading shoes with Sara for part of the way, each of them taking turns being one-shoed for part of the way. Sharing a shoe, now that was true friendship! And of course, just having Sara there with her when she tried to explain to the practical Greta, how she happened to come home with just one shoe, cemented their friendship even further. Greta pitched a royal fit when Leslie explained that she had lost one of the suede Capezio loafers she had begged Greta to buy her even though they were way too expensive. "But all the cool girls in school have a pair." It was hard enough to have a stylish look when you had to wear a uniform, so she and Sara loved to shop for shoes. And luckily, they wore the same size, so they could borrow each other's shoes. And since Sara went to the public school down the street from St. Monica's, no one knew that they each only owned half the shoes they wore to school.

She and Sara were still friends although they now lived almost three thousand miles away from each other. But the marvels of email and the Internet allowed them to share photos of grandchildren, the latest jokes about middle-aged women, and their mutual interest in nature. And it had been Sara who had flown to Nevada with Leslie to look for a home, even though she thought Leslie must be out of her mind for wanting to live in this desolate, God-forsaken place, so far from what Sara considered civilization. Sara had commented, as the 757 flew over Nevada, that she couldn't imagine why anyone would want to live in such a barren, brown state. To this day, every time Sara flew into the Reno airport for a visit, she reminded Leslie that she knew, looking out the windows, when they had reached Leslie's "beautiful brown Nevada" and she thanked God for her own lush green lawn and colorful gardens. Leslie wondered what Sara would say when she told her about her trip to Rome and all that had happened to her over the last six months. She was reluctant about telling anyone, even her own family, about her recent experiences. She was always thought to be a little bit off the wall, even by her own family, and this new turn in her life would engrave that picture even further into their thoughts. Except for George. Good old George would understand; he always did. And of course, now that he was a Cardinal, she needed his guidance even more than she had as a child. She sometimes thought George was the only one who really understood her. Well, we would see if he could understand any of this. If anyone could make sense of what was happening to her, George could.

George had even seemed to understand her fascination with cowboys. When other girls were dreaming about being nurses and teachers, or maybe even doctors or senators, Leslie's idea was to learn to rope and ride so she could be a cowboy. Saturday afternoons would find her at the matinee spaghetti westerns wearing her six shooters and cowboy boots. Instead of the carousel and other brightly lit midway rides at the county fair, she always headed first to the pony rides.

George had laughed when she told him that being a cow*girl* was no fun at all because they always seemed to be waiting back at the ranch while the cowboys were out saving the day, running the bad guys out of town and rounding up stray dogies.

When she was twelve, Leslie discovered the Bookmobile run by the local library. It stopped just across from her faithful gnarled oak tree on Maple Street, and Leslie spent all her free time on rainy summer days, especially when Sara was helping her mother out in her beauty shop, reading the books about the West she had checked out. She was ecstatic when she read about high-spirited women like Calamity Jane, Jessie Fremont, Nellie Cashman, and others. It was through these stories that she learned that all the cowgirls didn't just sit around back at the ranch waiting for their men; on the contrary, there were quite a few of them who went out and made things happen. It was these women who were drawing Leslie to the West. She knew from the time she read these stories that she would get there someday, by hook or by crook. The same year she read her first cowgirl story, she saw *Westward the Women* one Saturday afternoon at the matinee and it quickly became her "all time favorite movie ever." At twelve, that may not have been a great recommendation for the movie, but at 55, it was still her favorite, and she watched it over and over again, especially after Michael died. Watching those women haul the covered wagons over the most treacherous mountains became her salve for the open wounds caused by Michael's untimely departure from her life. It was just a month after his accident that she made the decision that would change her life forever, and the lives of more people than she could possibly dream. She would head west!

The flight attendant was back with fruit and cheese. Deciding against another glass of wine, Leslie opted for a cup of hot herbal tea to soothe her. She pulled an Egyptian chamomile from her stash of special, caffeine-free tea bags and a packet of Stevia sweetener from her carry-on bag. The movement of setting up their trays and passing drinks gave the businessman in the next seat the opportunity to make small talk with Leslie. She had removed her earphones, letting them fall about her neck. The man had no idea that she would not sleep at all on this flight and that the earphones were mainly to try to keep out the emanations coming from him and the other passengers.

"Are you going to Rome on business or pleasure?" his conversation began [*what's an attractive woman like you doing traveling to Europe by yourself?*]

"A little of both," Leslie replied. "I have some family business with my brother who lives there."

The Italian smiled. "Are you staying long?" Leslie easily heard his real request ["*Any chance we could get together while you're visiting our fair city?*"]

She sensed his nervousness about approaching her but knew his anxiety was based on the fact that this might be his last chance to seduce her before she closed her eyes and went back to her iPod. Leslie thought about Anne Rice's Vampire Lestat and how he sometimes felt he would lose his mind because of the thoughts of all the mortals within his range converging on him. She knew exactly how that fictional character felt. She herself had been barraged with voices and thoughts for the past several months. The Italian, Leslie noticed, was rubbing his Gucci loafers on the pant leg of his Armani suite, trying to assure that he was freshly polished before he moved in for the kill. No one, she thought, preened like the Italians. She was sure he had popped a breath mint in his mouth while she was preoccupied in her own thoughts.

"Has your brother lived in Rome long?" he went on. [*Is there a man in your life, besides your brother?*]

"Several years, but he studied there for many years, so he considers himself a Roman." Leslie thought it must now be obvious to the Italian that her brother was associated with the Church and that she had no interest in continuing the conversation, but he went on anyway.

"My name is Vittorio," he said, extending his hand. Of course this meant Leslie had to respond with a handshake and her name despite the fact that she knew what he was really saying was, [*once I touch her, she will feel my animal attraction*] "I've lived in Rome all my life, but visit New York frequently on business." [*Perhaps a long distance romance isn't out of the question*].

"I try to avoid New York as much as I can. I'm a West Coast person myself," Leslie replied, trying to end the overture politely, but firmly.

"Los Angeles?" he went on, not one to give up easily.

"Carson City, Nevada," Leslie replied, certain that he had never heard of this small western town. Although she gave him the name of the capital city of Nevada, the address of her ranch was actually that of a much smaller town ten miles outside Carson City. Most Europeans knew nothing about Nevada except that it was the home of Las Vegas. Nevada, she thought, was the most underrated of the fifty states, but it may have been the state's low profile, except of course for Las Vegas, which was known worldwide, that had attracted Leslie to it.

Looking at her lime green silk slacks, matching cashmere sweater set and expensive leather shoes, Leslie wished she had opted to travel in her usual outfit—Wrangler jeans, cowboy boots and a western style shirt. She had changed her mind at the last minute, not wishing to cause any embarrassment for George when the limo driver came to pick her up, and selected something from her East Coast, suburban housewife wardrobe. After all, she should look like a Cardinal's sister, not a rough cowhand. If this slick Italian could see her maneuvering her Nissan X-Terra across the rough back roads of Nevada or riding her horse, Mancha, with her hair flying in the wind, her face dirty and her boots well worn, his ardor would probably cool considerably. But Nevada and Mancha would have to wait. The best she could do now was to close her eyes and retreat as best she could into the Native American CD she had loaded onto her iPod and think about that fateful day that had led to this trip.

Chapter 2

Bishop, California

That morning, six months earlier, had started a lot like many of her days in Nevada started. She rose early, packed her nightclothes and her few toiletries, slipped into her jeans and sweater, and checked out of the motel. Leslie had gotten accustomed to traveling light and the fact that she didn't wear much makeup helped her morning routine go rather quickly for a woman her age. She had never been one for using a lot of "gunk," as Michael called it, on her face. She showered with the natural, chemical free soap and shampoo she always carried with her, rubbed Burt's Bees Milk & Honey with Coconut on her feet, legs, arms and face, and swept a touch of heather eye shadow on her eyelids, dabbed on light pink lip gloss, towel-dried her shoulder-length, auburn hair, and off she went. Skipping breakfast, she grabbed the packs of almonds and raisins she had packed in little paper bags for munching in the car, polished off one of her favorite Gala apples and opened a bottle of ice-cold spring water while driving. She had wanted to get an early start because she knew the drive up to the Ancient Bristlecone Forest would be a long one and then there was a two-hour hike to the oldest of the bristlecone pines. Driving along Route 120, taking a back road instead of the 395 highway, on her way from home she was as enthralled, as she always was driving through the mountainous terrain. Seeing the giant rock piles on either side of the road, she was reminded of her love for geology. (She must sign up for that course at UNR on geology next semester). The formation of mountains and the many different types of rocks in the West were a source of constant amazement for Leslie.

Rounding a bend in the road, she spotted a lake that left her with a surreal sense of wonderment. The lake reflected a perfect mirror image of the mountains above it. Not like the usual blurred, almost impressionistic reflections cast in most bodies of water, this one looked as though someone had placed a huge mirror on the ground; the image was perfect, almost too perfect. She had to stop and photograph this phenomenon. Not a student of water biology, she was not sure what gave this lake that special quality. Perhaps it had a high content of mercury but, in Leslie's eyes, it was a gift from God that she had decided to take this route to Bishop. By the time Leslie had parked the car, walked to the lake, taken some photographs and spent some time in prayer and reflection, she found herself hungry and decided to take this opportunity to go back to the car, grab her mid-morning snack and head back to the lake. She carried with her enough food for almost all her meals. She was so glad that Andre, knowing how much she liked to take road trips, had bought her a rather unique going away gift when she left for Nevada, an Igloo plug in cooler to keep her food cold without the bother of ice. Taking the cooler into her hotel room and plugging it in overnight, she could travel all day and not have to worry about finding a restaurant. She had learned quickly that there were not too many healthy restaurants in rural Nevada, so this was the perfect gift. She could have her salad, fresh organic fruit and cold spring water ready whenever she grew hungry or thirsty. And she was always thirsty in the desert. How many times she said a quick prayer of thanks for Andre knowing this was a perfect gift for her. It raised a few eyebrows at her going away party, but Andre and she knew that it was the best gift she had received. Now, she grabbed a luscious red pear, a bag of organic baby carrots, and a pack of foil-packed tuna along with her favorite Indian blanket, bought during her visit to New Mexico when she was in college. Sitting on the blanket by the lake, she opened her journal and wrote her reflections of this moment. Leslie enjoyed writing for herself even more than she did writing for profit.

She had been pleased to find out that she could actually make a nice living writing for travel magazines. After Michael died, she hadn't thought about how living without his paycheck would affect her, but she had made a small profit when she sold Valerie and Gary the house in West Hartford, enough to buy her little ranch and sock away enough money in mutual funds to provide her with a modest income. Added to the insurance proceeds and Michael's retirement fund, she had more than enough money to survive. But, she somehow felt that she didn't want to live on Michael's money. She thought that money really belonged to the children. She wanted to earn some money of her own and there was always that dream of becoming really rich and famous that she had inherited from her father. Leslie's income from her writing actually left her in a financial position almost equal to her status before Michael's death. When she had her first article published in *Sunset* magazine, she had been surprised to find that people enjoyed reading her travel stories almost as much as she enjoyed writing them. It seemed somehow unfair to the many people who worked so hard to make a living that she could earn money from something she enjoyed so much. When she wasn't writing for profit, she kept a journal of her own spiritual journey. And often, her journal reflections became part of the travel stories she wrote.

This trip was actually planned so she could write about her trip to the Ancient Bristlecone Forest for the AAA Magazine *Via*. Leslie, with her lifelong love for trees, had developed a magical attraction for the bristlecone pines as soon as she had heard about them, and the more she read about them, the more fascinated she became. Their existence on this earth after thousands of years was truly a miracle, and their survival strategies intrigued her. She thought about how much humanity could learn from the survival of these trees. The experts said they survived partly because they were in an alkaline environment. Leslie had done considerable research on the acidity/alkaline properties of the human body and was convinced, as were many nutritional experts, that keeping one's body in an alkaline PH balance could prevent cancer. Another reason for the trees' survival was that, although they grew in groves, they stood fairly far apart from each other. Leslie had always believed that a certain amount of distance between people was a good thing for survival. Even though she and Michael had a great marriage and a wonderful relationship, they each had their separate interests and had always felt free to pursue those interests apart from each other. She was convinced that this led to the longevity and intense satisfaction of their marriage. The scientists also found that the oldest of the trees lived on the tree line, where conditions were the harshest, and Leslie was certain that adversity made a person, or a tree, stronger. The harsh environment in which these trees lived had the benefit of helping them avoid fire, insects and other things that led to destruction. Their survival reminded Leslie of her grandparents who, she was convinced, survived and grew stronger because of the harshness of their lives. It was a proven fact that these trees put more energy into surviving than they did into growing; they were not large considering their age, the tallest being about 60 feet, dwarfed by the sequoias and giant redwoods of coastal California. Leslie had always tried to convey that message to her children that being the biggest, or the smartest, or the richest wasn't important, but internal strength was the thing that mattered.

The stop to meditate by the lake caused a delay in Leslie's plans, but it was well worth it. She was beginning to feel that there was something totally unique about this trip, about this landscape. She had been so intrigued with the lake, the mountains, and her journaling, that she lost track of time. She realized that it would be late by the time she got to the bristlecone trees, so she had decided she'd better spend the night in Bishop and then head to the Bristlecone Forest. But as Leslie was prone to do, she also got sidetracked in Bishop, stopping to visit some fascinating little shops there. The smells of the bakery enticed her, even though she would not eat any of those sugar-laden goodies. She knew most travel readers preferred to read about quaint little shops and specialty restaurants than about trees, so she had to have some local color in her stories. In fact, when she finally arrived at the Bristlecone Forest, she was crushed when she realized she wouldn't be able to see Methuselah, the oldest living thing on Earth, because there was a four-hour round trip hike to the grove of trees where Methuselah stood. And she only had this one day before she had to get back to her ranch because her ranch hand was leaving town and would not be there to feed the horses. What a disappointment this trip would be. She had waited for years to see these trees, ever since she had heard about them and found out that the only place in the world that they existed was in six states in the United States. Although there were plenty of bristlecone pines to see along the road on the way to the ranger station, she had really wanted to see the prize of them all—Methuselah.

Leslie felt disappointed, as she had when she and Michael had tried to visit the bristlecone pines in Great Basin National Park, near Ely, Nevada, on their trip there one Memorial Day weekend, but the late snowfall meant that the trails were covered with eight feet of snow and they could not fulfill this dream. Their side trip to the small town of Baker, however, lent them the opportunity to visit the ruins of an ancient Fremont Culture Indian village and they were able to visit the caves at the park and do some hiking on the trials that were not flooded due to the melting snow. And now, she was warned that the hike would take her into dusk, and that she would then have to descend the mountain in the gathering twilight. However, the middle-aged park ranger there suggested that she take the "short" drive to see the largest, if not the oldest, of the bristlecone pines, the Matriarch. Leslie was grateful to the woman for her suggestion, thinking that perhaps this trip wouldn't be wasted after all.

The drive, however, wasn't short, nor was it an easy one. It was nineteen miles on a dirt road and she wondered more than once if she should have just attempted the hike to Methuselah and taken her chances. Driving up that mountainous dirt road, she felt she would never see the end of it. It appeared to snake through endless hills and valleys, and cast a mirage-like deceptive feeling that the road got better in spots, until she got to those places and found it really wasn't any easier driving, just a different texture of dirt and stones. And along the way, were hundreds of beautiful, gnarled, windswept trees to fascinate her and she had to stop periodically and take a few photos. As she drove, a song echoed in her head, a song that she first remembered hearing at George's ordination. She wasn't sure of the title of the song, but the words were ringing over and over in her head—"surely the presence of the Lord is in this place." And she knew that this was truly a special place, a holy place. She remembered Psalm 24, one of her favorites, "who shall ascend the mountain of the Lord, and who shall stand in this holy place?" She felt like Moses, climbing to the Holy Ground of Mount Sinai. When she finally reached that fateful spot, the grove of trees that held the Matriarch, she was breathless and awe-struck by the deathly silence that was like nothing she had ever experienced. She was at the top of the world and she spent at least ten minutes just taking it all in before she saw her destiny. There it was, the Matriarch, a thing that was alive when Moses walked the earth! Could it really be?

As she climbed out of her X-Terra, she was compelled to pull off her boots, although the temperature was quite chilly at this altitude; she knew that she was indeed on Holy Ground. There was not another soul in sight. While she had passed two cars making the return trip, there were none here now. Leslie knew what it must feel like to be the last survivor on Earth. A chill ran up her spine, not so much because of her bare feet and the cool ground. It was more like that feeling she got at the top of the Ferris wheel when it stopped at the top, a feeling that if she could overcome her fear she could jump out of the car and fly. Placing her cowboy boots in the car, she trod carefully over the rocks; what if there were scorpions up here? And yet, she knew she had to approach the Matriarch barefooted and thought for a minute she might even strip off all her clothes and face this moment naked. Only the thought that perhaps there might be cars behind her stopped her from doing this. Barefoot would have to do!

She walked slowly, thoughtfully, reverently toward the tree that, although unmarked for fear of vandalism, Leslie knew to be the Matriarch. The walk to the Matriarch reminded Leslie of her barefoot walk through the labyrinth in Boulder City, a walk on holy ground.

She thought she should probably have taken her camera with her, but somehow it seemed profane to even think about photographing the Matriarch. She thought of the Amish she used to see when she visited George in Pennsylvania. They did not allow their pictures to be taken. And of the tales of the Old-West Indians who thought their souls would be stolen if they allowed themselves to be captured in the White Man's box. She somehow knew that the tree would not want Leslie to take her picture. Leslie felt drawn to the Matriarch in a way she couldn't understand, but she felt its power emanating towards her, drawing her in. She was almost afraid to get too close because she felt she might become part of the tree, and remain trapped there forever. As she got closer, the power seemed to be calling her name and she thought surely this was the God who called out to Moses in the burning bush, "I AM WHO AM."

She was close enough to touch the tree now and yet she held back. She couldn't explain this chilling fear that ran through her, but she somehow knew that touching this tree would change her life forever. It became clear to her, as she was within inches of the trunk, that she would soon be touching God. She felt something brush over her foot, perhaps a leaf, perhaps an insect, but it didn't matter. The thoughts of scorpions were far from her mind now. Nothing was on Leslie's mind except the three inches that separated her fingertips from the tree. She might have been standing there for a few seconds or an hour. She had lost all track of time, but she knew she couldn't hesitate forever; she had to fulfill her destiny. And touch God she would.

Chapter 3

Backwards in Time

As her fingers closed that three-inch gap, she felt something like electricity coming from the tree. Heat, warmth, fire; it was beginning to fill her soul. Then her fingers were on the bark, the smooth living bark. In a heartbeat, she was enveloped in something beyond human comprehension. She felt as though she were falling, like those dreams she used to have as a child where she felt she was suspended in space, and then falling but falling gently, without fear. Her head was spinning. Stars seemed to be bursting forth from the nothingness, glowing brightly and then dimming again. And suddenly, she was in her mother's arms. She was just days old and she could feel Greta's warm body comforting her. And she understood Greta's inexplicable joy at having a daughter. Funny, she had never realized this bond while Greta was alive. In fact, he had always suspected that Greta, like many mothers, who seemed to love their sons more than their daughters, was closer to George than she would ever be to Leslie. Leslie had always thought it was because George had his mother's personality, while she had Henry's, that Greta seemed to respect George more. But now a new revelation was manifesting itself in Leslie. She felt, for the first time, her mother's deep love for her, and sensed a strength in her mother that surpassed even the knowledge of the strength that Leslie knew while Greta was living. Suddenly, Greta seemed almost superhuman in her strength. Perhaps it was because Leslie felt so weak and helpless in her mother's arms, but it seemed even more than this. It was as though Leslie, even as a baby in her mother's arms was receiving the strength that Greta was pouring out to her, and she realized for the first time how much of her mother's power actually existed within her own spirit.

And then, in what seemed like an instant, but could have been years, Leslie was watching her grandmother, Petra, in her modest cottage in Germany. Petra had led a grueling life, growing up on a farm, the oldest of thirteen children, raising her twelve siblings after her mother died in childbirth having her thirteenth child, Gerhard.

Petra's father, Heinrich, took to drinking after his wife Anna's death, and Petra had to not only dodge his wrath, but protect her brothers and sisters from Heinrich's angry ravings which, on more than one occasion, resulted in physical violence. He particularly chose Gerhard, the youngest, as the object of his wrath, blaming him for Anna's death. Heinrich vacillated between thoughts of suicide and finding an attractive young woman to raise his children. But then, Petra could handle that job, and Heinrich wouldn't have to deal with courtship, marriage and having another woman to satisfy. It seemed easier to just let things go on as they were, with Petra running the household and Heinrich losing himself in the bottle. At fifteen, Petra should have been having friends her own age, giggling with girlfriends and thinking about her first kiss instead of changing diapers, chasing after two sets of twins, and helping the older children with their schoolwork. It was no wonder that when Petra had her opportunity to escape with the farmhand whom Heinrich had hired, she grabbed that opportunity and eloped with Samuel. Heinrich was devastated, not so much by concern that his daughter was making a mistake, but by the thought of being left to raise twelve children by himself. He solved his dilemma by relying on some of the neighbor women and his next-oldest daughter, Gertrude, to raise the children and went back to his drinking.

Petra, meanwhile, found her life not much improved financially. She and Samuel had to start their married life in the bunkhouse of the small farm on which Samuel found work. However, she and Samuel were madly in love, and despite everyone thinking that she married Samuel just to get away from Heinrich and the demands of running the Frier household, their marriage was one built on a solid love for one another. Samuel was gentle, frugal and hardworking. He soon worked his way up to be the foreman on the ranch and had saved enough money to buy the ranch when its owner, Friedrich, dropped dead in the field one day and his widow decided to pack up her children and go back to her family homestead. Samuel and Petra worked hard to build the farm into a profitable venture, and when they had saved enough money, immigrated to the United States not long after Greta was born and settled in upstate New York.

Leslie had always felt a special relationship with Petra. From early childhood, she thanked God for having her maternal grandmother living close by. Many were the times she and Sara would walk to Petra's house for some of her homemade stollen, gingerbread cookies or other goodies. Especially when Leslie was mad at Greta for being too harsh, Petra was always there with some kind words that were as easy to swallow as the coconut custard for which Petra was famous. It seemed Petra always had something in the oven that smelled wonderful and tasted even better. Greta was a good cook too, but there was something abut Petra's house that fascinated Leslie, and the other neighborhood children as well. Her grandmother came to be know as "Aunt Petra" to the whole neighborhood. She was always ready to take a fresh raisin pie, which Petra called "funeral pie," to a neighbor for a wake; feed the scruffy little kids who magically showed up at her door just about the time a fresh batch of lebkuchen was coming out of the oven; or nurse anyone in the family or neighborhood who was sick. She didn't even seem to mind when the neighborhood kids tracked dirt on her shiny linoleum floor that was literally clean enough to "eat off of." She would just scrub it again after the kids left. And Petra had dozens of old world remedies that seemed to work better that all the antibiotics in the pharmacy. Even though Leslie recoiled at the taste of some of those remedies, she had to admit they worked. The horehound cough drops Petra found in the market worked much better than all the drugstore remedies the other kids in school took for their sore throats. And teas—Petra must have had a hundred different brews, one for every ailment imaginable! She had one she gave Leslie when she had menstrual cramps, one for headaches, one for sore throats, one for constipation, or any other malady that struck her family. Although the kids in school made fun of her for using all those old wives' remedies, Leslie was proud to say she got through six years of elementary school without a single absence, and she credited Petra and her old world remedies for that. How thrilled Leslie was to see, many years later, that Petra's advice was becoming popular with the younger generation. All the stores were filled with those special teas, and there were dozens of advertorials on TV about using natural remedies to cure or prevent just about anything.

But Leslie had never known anything about Petra's life in Germany; it was something she had never spoken about, at least not with Leslie or George. Now it seemed Leslie was standing at the window of Petra and Samuel's meager little cottage and Leslie was enthralled as she watched her grandparents as Samuel delivered Greta, who turned out to be their only child. There was no money and no time for a doctor. This was something Samuel had to do on his own. Even though he was barely nineteen, he seemed to have a calm and experienced touch. Perhaps it was all those years as a farmhand, delivering horses, sheep, and cows, but Samuel seemed to know exactly what to say to Petra to make the delivery easier. And when Greta finally emerged, he cleaned her gently and cut the cord with a steady hand. As he placed Greta on Petra's chest, the two of them looked into each other's eyes, and their prayer was unspoken, but they each knew it was a mutual prayer. Greta would grow up in the United States and have a better life than the meager one Samuel and Petra had known as children. As Leslie 'watched' this scene, she was amazed to see that the look on Petra's face was one she had seen before, one that had always fascinated her. It was the look on the face of Jesus in a painting she had once seen in museum somewhere. Although she couldn't remember where, she remembered the haunting look on El Greco's *Head of Christ*. Those eyes, filled with sadness and joy at the same time, yearning to go home and yet bound to do what He was sent to earth to accomplish, calling out to Leslie, to the world to listen. Those eyes were reflected now in Petra who had the determination to accomplish something she was destined to do, sadness at leaving her homeland, yet joyful at what the new world would hold for her, and knowing that she had a calling that went beyond being a good wife to Samuel and a wise mother for Greta. She knew there was something more in her destiny, something in her lineage that would change the world.

Chapter 4

Farther Back in Time

For a brief moment, Leslie came back to the present and became aware that she was in the 21st century and that she was now clinging to the tree, every inch of her body pressing against the smooth bark. In fact, she felt that she was entwined so tightly with the tree that she had actually entered into it. She was pretty sure that she was actually several inches into the tree and she thought perhaps she should pull away, lest she become permanently trapped within the Matriarch. And yet, she knew she had to go on, to enter further into this mystery that was absorbing her. She breathed deeply, closed her eyes and was once again back in time, watching now as Anna, Petra's mother was scratching in the dirt, trying to force the withering crops on her farm in eastern Poland to grow. Anna was just eight years old, but the family depended on her to feed them, now that her older brothers were off to the Great War and her father was too sick to manage their meager little farm. Anna's mother, Katrina, had died in childbirth, leaving Anna to care for her younger stepsiblings and her father. Anna did the best she could with the farm and managed to keep the chickens laying enough eggs to sell to neighboring farms. She went into town every Friday to sell the eggs that she didn't feed to her younger brothers and sisters. Most of the townspeople felt sorry enough for Anna to buy a few eggs that they didn't really need or let her trade them for a bit of ham or bacon, knowing it would probably be the only meat the little Kowalczek children would taste that month. Anna longed to kill some of the chickens so she could make some soup for her little family, but she knew she couldn't afford the loss of the eggs. She only killed the chickens after they were too old to lay eggs. In her childish innocence, she thought that perhaps the chicken soup could make her father well again, well enough to share the responsibilities of raising the family left behind by Katrina that cold February day when the youngest, Stanley, came into the world. Despite the sadness that filled Anna's heart every time she looked at

Stanley, knowing that their father blamed him for Katrina's death, he was Anna's favorite. She had been the only "mother" he had ever known and he clung to her at every waking moment, even following her into the chicken coop to try to help gather the eggs. Of course, had Anna let him help, he would have dropped too many of the precious eggs, leaving even less money to feed the family. Anna was determined that Stanley would grow up healthy and feeling loved by her, if not by his father. As Stanley grew, Anna taught him his lessons. He loved learning and became a prolific reader, although getting books was almost impossible in war-torn Poland.

The Germans were merciless and, though many Poles were wearing the German uniform, most of the men in Anna's village were fighting for the Russians in this war that seemed to her like it would go on for thousands of years. The one consolation in Anna's unhappy life was that all of their neighbors were in the same state as her family, so they didn't look down on her and her siblings. Although they felt sorry for Anna, being the mother, father and teacher for the younger ones, they respected her for trying so hard to take care of her family and for teaching not only herself but her younger brothers and sisters to read and write, something most of the villagers couldn't do themselves. Before long, people in the village were coming to Anna asking her to read letters for them and write to their sons, brothers and lovers who were fighting the Germans. Anna dreamed about becoming a teacher and setting up her own little school in the village. Perhaps the parish priest would help her.

However, Anna's dream of running a school would never happen. Although the war was technically over, the Germans were still there and just as nasty as ever. Anna felt they would stay forever. By the time Anna was thirteen, she knew she could never leave her father and her family, especially Stanley. She learned to sew and make delicate lace and was beginning to make quite a name for herself in the village. The woman of the village who could still afford to buy fine things came to Anna for their babushkas and tablecloths as well as to have their letters read and written. The Easter that Anna could actually buy new shoes for her brothers, was probably the happiest time of her young life. She even managed to scrape together enough for a new felt hat and cotton to make a new shirt for Stanley. He looked so proud at midnight mass that Anna thought she could never be happier.

Two year later, she found happiness in a most unexpected place. While walking to church one day, she was accosted in the street by four of the more brutal German soldiers who had pretty much taken over the town. They were taunting her and making lewd remarks. She tried to cross the street to get away from them, but they grabbed her coat and started pulling at her long blond braids. She knew what was going to happen next and she was more terrified than she had ever been in her young life. She prayed for an avenging angel to come down from the heavens, riding a white horse and wielding a sword, as in the legend of St. George slaying the dragon. When the sword appeared, however, it was not an angel or St. George who wielded it, but rather a German lieutenant, not much older than the four hooligans who surrounded her. When her attackers scattered, she began to recover enough to raise her head, and found herself looking into the most beautiful blue eyes she had ever seen. How could someone with such gentle eyes be one of the murderous barbarians she knew these German soldiers to be?

Anna had found the love of her life, even more precious than her darling Stanley was to her. Franz Fehr was the gentle lover Anna had always dreamed about and when she found herself pregnant with his child, she knew she would follow him back to Germany, even if it meant leaving behind her beloved family. But she couldn't leave Stanley behind. She begged Franz to take him with them and, amazingly, he agreed. Starting married life in a new country, with a strange language and even stranger religion was not easy for Anna, but somehow, having eight-year-old Stanley with her, seemed to help. Stanley learned German faster than Anna did and repaid all the years of Anna's kindness to him by teaching her to read and write in German. Anna even gave up her beloved church and became a Lutheran.

It was after Anna had moved to Germany and married Franz that she started thinking more and more about her mother. Maybe it was because she was going to be a mother herself that she started longing for her own mother. She wished Katrina could be here to see the birth of her child, to cuddle and coo to her child as only a grandmother could do. But she somehow knew that Katrina would be looking down on her, would be holding her hand as she groaned in labor, and would be gently kissing the newborn baby in Anna's arms as soon as it was born. With that sixth sense that pregnant women sometimes seem to have, Anna started conversing with her mother in her head. She thought for a while that she might be losing her mind. She had heard that sometimes pregnancy and childbirth did strange things to women.

The conversations with her mother seemed to grow as the child within her womb grew. Katrina was telling her to not be afraid, that she would not suffer the same fate that Katrina had during childbirth. Katrina was also telling her how to raise her daughter. She knew now, through Katrina's assurances, that she would have a beautiful, healthy daughter, and that she would name her Petra, the rock that would hold her steady throughout the her lifetime. Anna remembered a story like this from her childhood—yes, it was the story of the Virgin Mary being assured by the angel Gabriel not to worry—that she was carrying the Son of God. Anna felt that she indeed was carrying a very special child and that this child would bear an even more special child, and that with each new birth, their lineage would grow stronger, and more spiritual, and someday, her blood line would reach perfection.

Chapter 5

Eastern Europe and Asia

Katrina was proud of her Russian heritage. Her grandmother had immigrated to Poland, but was always Russian in her heart as her daughter Georgiana and her granddaughter Katrina were. Katrina grew up in what would someday be called an upper middle-class family, her mother, Georgiana, and her grandmother, Natalie, both being merchants of fine cloth. Although not aristocracy themselves, they were well acquainted with the ways of royalty through their clients and lived their lives as though they were members of the royal family themselves. They closed their shop every afternoon at 3 p.m. and had strong Russian tea and chrust chycki or other Polish pastries, not being able to secure their native Russian delicacies here in Poland. Although their economic situation and shrewd business sense forced them to save the finest of their cloths for their paying customers, they always managed to salvage enough fabric to make themselves gowns to rival those of the finest women in the city. They learned to do fancy needlework. They planted amazing gardens that not only provided healthy meals but an array of wonderfully-colored and sweet-scented flowers to fill their home. They worked hard all day, but their evening hours were spent in much the same way as the idle rich spent their evenings—entertaining musicians and poets—although their guests were the "starving artists" and not the well established composers and poets of the royalty.

The Petroff women could easily have passed for aristocracy—they spoke well, knew all about art and music, and were genteel women. One walking into their shop would pick them out as customers, not as the shopkeepers. Their funds were meager in comparison to their clientele, but they could stretch a zloty further than anyone in their town. Katrina followed in their footsteps. She learned at an early age how to dress, how to speak, how to behave in public. Her mother kept the shop open extra hours to find money for voice lessons and she learned to play the piano by ear, even composing her own music. Katrina could have been a successful singer but she gave that idea up to marry at the age of nineteen. Katrina had met Gregor when she was seventeen and they immediately fell in love. When Gregor went off to the university, he begged Katrina to go along with him and she insisted she would only go if they were married. Although Gregor was not prepared to support a wife while he completed his studies in astronomy, Katrina explained that she could support them both with her sewing abilities, and she was right. So, off they went to Warsaw, he to study and she to open her own little shop, catering to the professors' wives. It wasn't long before she found herself with child. Her delicate frame was not ready for a child and it was difficult pregnancy. Gregor was at Katrina's' side when she gave birth to Anna. After the midwife laid Anna in Gregor's arms, she asked him to leave while she tried to stop the massive bleeding, but it was too late. Katrina, breathing the gift of life into Anna, gave up her own last breath with her rosary in her hand and Gregor's sweet kisses still on her cheek.

After Katrina's death, Gregor was forced to go back to the farm. There was no chance of him ever completing his work at the university now. He had not only lost the love of his life, but also the income from Katrina's shop, and now he had a baby to feed and care for as well. Had Gregor not been too proud to go to the Petroff's for help, he might have made a good life for himself and for Anna, but he couldn't possibly ask the Petroff women for help. First of all, they were Russian, and secondly, they were women. No, he would rather go back to his little farm and try to care for his daughter himself, with the help of cousins and neighbors. Of course Gregor hadn't counted on the war taking away all his family and most of his friends. And he certainly hadn't counted on getting sick himself. He soon married a distant cousin so he would have someone to take care of Anna. Before long, he was the father of four more children, and the stepfather of four bothers, all of who would soon go off to fight the Germans.

Anna grew up fast, becoming the mother to Gregor's new wife's children after she also died in childbirth. The loss of a second wife in childbirth was too much for Gregor to handle and he soon became sick himself, leaving Anna the head of the household. But Katrina was always on Gregor's mind, even while he was making love to his new wife, Stella, and when the midwife laid little Francis in his arms, it was Katrina he thought of, not Stella. These last four children should have been his and Katrina's. Through the years he spent mourning Katrina, she was always there with him, and he knew she was with Anna as well. They never talked about it, but they both somehow knew that the other was also hearing Katrina's voice in their head, felt her breath on them at night when they slept and they both prayed every day for Katrina to help them survive.

Leslie was now totally absorbed into the Matriarch but she was no longer afraid of being trapped within the tree. She knew she had to go on and that there was a mystery here that she had to learn and had to use this knowledge somehow. She felt a special kinship to Katrina and to Petra, and she was becoming aware of a pattern to the revelation she was experiencing. She realized that she was tracing her ancestry but only through the women of the family. And she knew that these women she had "met" shared a gift for being intuitive, strong and faithful. She wasn't sure yet what this meant, but she knew she needed to go further back and the answers would be there.

She was suddenly riding bareback on a horse with the young Katrina. It was a solid black stallion with a white star on its forehead. Georgiana had taught Katrina to ride at an early age, perhaps because it was part of the trappings of the aristocracy and Georgiana wanted her daughter to feel like she was royalty. However, Katrina early on discarded the genteel sidesaddle riding of the titled ladies in favor of riding bareback. Katrina rode like a man; after all she had Cossack blood flowing through her veins. Georgiana would have preferred seeing her daughter ride in the manner of a lady, but she knew that Katrina was headstrong and that she would ride the way she wanted to ride, her hair flying in the wind. Sharing this moment with Katrina riding across the steppes of Poland, Leslie felt totally at home. She felt as though she were riding her own Leopard Appaloosa, Mancha, so named because of his "many spots," the literal translation of his name.

Mancha was Leslie's favorite of her four horses. Although he was not the most beautiful of the horses and certainly not the most valuable, she and Mancha had always had a very special relationship. Although Mancha was a gelding, he behaved like a stallion, protecting the mares in his stable and challenging the stallions if they got too close to the mares. Mancha had challenged Leslie at first too, but once she let him know who was boss, they got along splendidly. She had always felt an inexplicable special closeness to Mancha and could spend hours on the trails with him while she usually grew tired after a morning riding any of the three quarter horses she owned. Leslie understood perfectly the relationship between Katrina and her stallion, Romani.

Katrina was a young girl, younger than Leslie had been when she learned to ride, but she handled the horse like a well-seasoned equestrian. She had a way with horses, a way learned from generations of Cossacks. Leslie was aware that her connection with her own horse was a strange juxtaposition of Katrina's experience. It was after a long, happy life with Michael, that she felt the freedom and solace of riding her horse. Katrina's carefree days on horseback, on the other hand, preceded a life of hard work cut short by her early demise.

Chapter 6

Back to North America

Countless millennia had passed before Leslie's eyes in what could have been seconds, minutes or hours. Leslie was now back in time thousands of years and was watching a young native girl whom she knew to be another of her ancestors. She realized for the first time that she had witnessed every female ancestor between Greta and this young girl. The young native girl was named, Dukh Asyuhayee, *Spirit of the Tree*, and was of the Tlingit tribe. Dukh Asyuhayee was cleaning fish caught by her father off the coast of what is now known as Sitka, Alaska. She was using an ulu, the rounded blade used by the natives to clean, chop, slice and mash food in a small wooden bowl. Although her father was the chief, she worked as hard as any of the other girls in the village. She was of the House of Raven and was required to marry a boy from the House of the Eagle, as was the custom of the Tlingit. She knew her father had already picked out a handsome, strong young man for her and she was ready to start her own home. The Tlingit were matrilineal and so their children would also be of the House of Raven. When the new moon appeared, her father would host a potlatch to announce the marriage of his daughter to Kugun Khugoos, Bright Cloud. Dukh Asyuhayee's family had been living and fishing along the shore for many thousands of years and would exist there many more thousands of years, although some of her people would migrate to the "New World," Russia. She was one of those who would give up the life she had know since her birth and follow her husband to seek his riches in a new land.

Kugun Khugoos was not content to fish forever. Although he was grateful to Dukh Asyuhayee's father for choosing him from the many strong young men in the tribe to marry his only daughter, he was not content to live under the shadow of his father-in-law. He and Dukh Asyuhayee would make a life of their own in this new land. Soon Dukh Asyuhayee and Kugun Khugoos would join the many people traveling westward over the landmass that stretched between what is now Russia and what is now Alaska. Along the way, they would pass Asians traveling eastward to what *they* considered to be the new world.

Leslie was brought back to the present for a moment, realizing that this pilgrimage had always been thought to flow only eastward. It seemed to Leslie that even then, there was the 'grass is greener' attitude, but she still didn't fully comprehend what this two-way traffic across the narrow land mass meant.

As Leslie 'watched' Dukh Asyuhayee and Kugun Khugoos found their way, after weeks on foot over the frozen tundra, to a small village where they decided to settle, not because they were warmly welcomed or because the village was much better than the one they had left, but because they were tired and too weary to think about going much farther. They were in a new land and would make their own family. It made no difference to the people of this small frozen village that Dukh Asyuhayee's father had been chief in her land. Nor did it make any difference that they had left their village against her father's wishes. It didn't even matter so much that Kugun Khugoos was young and strong and would make a good warrior should the need arise to defend their village. What mattered most to these simple people was that there were two more mouths to feed, but also two more sets of hands to work. If the need to feed these two new strangers outweighed the benefits of their work, they would be driven from the village to make their way to the next settlement. But that would not happen. Dukh Asyuhayee and Kugun Khugoos made sure of that. Although before long, there was another mouth to feed, and then another soon after that, Dukh Asyuhayee and Kugun Khugoos were hard workers and quickly became valued citizens of the village. Kugun Khugoos, being a skilled fisherman and hunter, taught the men of the village how to make better tools for hunting and fishing and even taught them his native language, which they found useful when conversing with traveling Tlingit who had often in the past tricked them into bad trades. And, Dukh Asyuhayee likewise taught the women of the village how to weave baskets that were so tight they could be used to boil water and cook soup. And the women were fascinated by the beautiful blankets and robes Dukh Asyuhayee was able to produce and begged her to show them how to sew these wondrous treasures.

It wasn't long before Kugun Khugoos was selected as the leader of the village, and Dukh Asyuhayee was right beside him in helping the village council make important decisions. Her strength and intelligence were unrivaled by anything the village women had ever seen. They had been basically a lazy and not very bright people until these strangers taught them new skills and regaled them with stories of their journey, their homeland and the villages there, which were far advanced in every way. If these people had the ambition to set up a more sophisticated political structure, and create a state of their own, they would surely have made Kugun Khugoos and Dukh Asyuhayee king and queen. They believed that Dukh Asyuhayee had supernatural powers and perhaps they were correct in this assumption. She certainly was able to heal with special herbs and prayers and she had an uncanny gift when it came to sensing trouble. Many of the villagers brought their newborn children to Dukh Asyuhayee to receive her blessing and they turned to her when they needed counsel or just needed another woman to listen to them. When she told them what her name meant in the Tlingit language, they understood why she seemed to have a strange gift for communing with nature and for using the bark, leaves and flowers from various trees to cure all sorts of ailments. She really did have a spirit of the tree within her.

Leslie felt that she finally understood her own passion for trees and her special gift for communing with nature as she came to realize that she was now almost fully within the Matriarch. It could have taken her hours, days or years to get to this point, but she felt it was a matter of minutes, maybe even seconds. Somewhere in the back of her mind, she thought she should have checked her watch as she approached the tree, but it didn't really matter. The only thing that mattered to Leslie now was getting to the center of it all. She knew that truth lay in the center of the Matriarch.

Chapter 7

Nevada Roots

The light and the warmth grew even stronger and Leslie knew she was getting closer. Another several thousand years flashed through her soul, again sensing and feeling every one of her female ancestors, until she was now in the heart of a small village of Paiute Indians in northern Nevada. They were cooking by fire on the shores of the magical place Leslie had been so entranced with on her trip with Michael—Pyramid Lake! Although the surroundings had changed some, Leslie was amazed that it looked almost identical to the way she had seen it several thousand years later. The great matriarch of the tribe, Woqobi Muguwa, *Spirit of the Tree*, was amazingly like her counterpart who lived more than a thousand years later, Dukh Asyuhayee. Woqobi Muguwa was also a highly skilled seamstress and had the power to heal and counsel those who came to her in need. She loved living so close to the lake because she knew it held a special healing power and she was able to use its power to work many wonders among her people.

Leslie could almost picture Woqobi Muguwa actually walking on the water, her power was so strong. In fact, many of the villagers feared her because of this great power. Some thought she must have an evil spirit inside her, but the elders of the tribe knew that the sprit inside Woqobi Muguwa was a godly one. They called on her when important decisions needed to be made, such as relocating the village. It had been Woqobi Muguwa who led them to the site by the lake, close to the pyramid like structure jutting out from its eastern shore. And this was the finest location the tribe had ever had for its village. The tribe was awed by their first site of the pyramid, and came to worship this unique structure, not certain if it was of human or divine origin, but sensing that there was power within it, a power that would be theirs if they dwelt close to the pyramid, if they respected it and if they protected it from marauding tribes who might seek to destroy it because of their fear.

Each morning, Woqobi Muguwa called the tribe to prayer facing the pyramid with the rising sun at their backs. Their prayers were for rain, for good crops, for peace within their tribe and protection from the tribes who might come to seek their land. Occasionally there were other tribes who came to see this wondrous structure they had heard tales about from travelers, and to see the tribe that was led by a woman. Some of these tribes were fierce and warlike. The Paiutes were a peaceful people who avoided confrontations with other tribes. One of the reasons for settling here by the lake was that it was not often visited by other tribes; it lacked the lush fertile soil to grow corn, and was often in danger because of droughts that came every year in late summer. When other tribes did wander close to the little community by the lake, they were welcomed if they came in peace. Woqobi Muguwa invited the visiting tribes to share prayer and meals with them and even gave them little gifts like baskets and hunting tools made by the men and women of her tribe. However, when these visiting tribes came with intentions that were not peaceful Woqobi Muguwa could be an imposing and formidable enemy. Those tribes who came to the Pyramid, thinking that a tribe ruled by a woman would not stand up and fight for their rights, were proved wrong almost immediately. Woqobi Muguwa could tell, even before they entered the camp, if their intentions were honorable or not. And those who thought they could overpower this small tribe were quickly sent running when they saw the weapons this tribe had devised. Although they never used them without provocation, they had sharpened stones which they used with slingshots. Their arrows were saturated with poisons that could kill within seconds. Although they had probably only used these weapons twice in the time Woqobi Muguwa had led them, enemies were often given a demonstration of their power by having one of the best marksman shoot a jack rabbit or a small deer before the visiting strangers could even see it. Once the animal was retrieved and they saw that it had been paralyzed the instant the poison entered its system, they were reluctant to make any trouble for the Paiutes. Woqobi Muguwa had found this poison which, if mixed with the water from the lake and given in small doses, could cure many ailments, but if administered in its pure form would kill a grown man in about five seconds. Only the foolish would try to conquer this tribe led by a woman!

Leslie regained her presence of mind enough to realize that she held within herself a part of all the women she had seen in this vision.

She had Petra's strength of character and ambition; she had Katrina's love for horses and her way of becoming one with the horse; she had the sprit of adventure that she found in Dukh Asyuhayee; and she had the healing touch and powerful leadership skills of Woqobi Muguwa. She wondered if all people had this magical mingling of all their ancestors qualities, or if was something unique to her family, but she knew that she held something of all of these women within her own sprit. She suddenly had the realization that Valerie would hold all of this, plus whatever gift Leslie would bequeath to her and she was overjoyed knowing that this sprit would live on forever through Valerie's heirs.

Chapter 8

Creation

Leslie was now back much farther in time, she wasn't sure how many millennia had passed before her, how many generations, but the western part of the United States was still covered with the waters of the Great Basin and life was just beginning to emerge from the water. She knew that she was back farther than she could ever imagine and that she was now very close to the center of the tree. In fact, she thought she might have entered its very core, but yet, there was more to come, she was sure. And, indeed, there was much more! She suddenly realized that she was now back billions of years in time and she was witnessing creation itself. Yes, she was touching God. She could hear God's voice and feel God's touch. She watched and listened as she saw and heard and felt the entire universe being birthed from the womb of God. She felt the warmth, was blinded by the light of the sun. She drifted in the waters of creation, and then she was moving forward again as she stood on the bridge between Heaven and the Earth that came many billions of years later. And she watched life crawl out of the waters. It was becoming clear to her now. That creation of humankind was happening simultaneously in many different worlds all over the universe. It was also clear to her that God was Mother and Father of all of this.

And she understood that in the beginning it was the female creation that understood the mind of God better than the male. The world was created peaceful and loving, and would probably have remained so had not humankind used its God-given free will to defy what it knew to be true—that creation was a gift from God and that the highest form of this creation—humankind—was meant to steward and guide the world as loving parent, not to use it up and dominate it, and she wondered how humankind's interpretation of creation had become so warped.

She understood that the Parent God created humankind in God's own image and humankind was meant to be parent to each other and to all of creation. But it had all gone awry—how or why, Leslie wasn't sure, but she understood that this was not how it was meant to be. Even when God sent prophets and mystics to reveal God's self to humankind, we didn't listen. And, the final insult, even when God came to earth in human form, humankind still rebelled and went its own way. And then, to make matters worse, humankind corrupted God's teachings by setting up its own rules and regulations, dividing the Church on Earth into so many factions, no one seemed to know what the will of God really was any more. And now here Leslie was, at the core of the universe, touching God, and hearing words that she knew she had to proclaim to any one who would listen. There were many thoughts unspoken, many questions she wanted to ask, and answers she wished she could somehow record so she wouldn't get anything wrong. But she knew she would recall the words God was speaking to her as though they were indelibly ingrained on her brain and in her heart.

"Honor and protect my creation.

Recognize and celebrate the diversity I birthed from my womb.

Return my church to the prophets and the mystics."

Leslie did not want to leave the tree; she wanted to cling to it and to this encounter with God forever. She recalled reading about people who had had near-death experiences and remembered that they all described a similar feeling, being drawn to the light and not wanting to return, but being told they must. As she reluctantly disengaged herself from the tree after what seemed like hours, but was probably only minutes, she thought about the whole experience of the afternoon; did it really all happen in a single afternoon or had she been there for days, weeks, an eternity? Although she had not checked her watch as she approached the tree, she knew from the location of the sun that it had been less than an hour and yet she had experienced an eternity.

She walked barefoot back to her X-Terra, slowly, reverently, and reluctantly. Although there was a chill in the air and the sun was getting low, she felt a strange warmth inside her, even though she had goose bumps on her arms. She sat for a few minutes on the front seat of her car, with her feet hanging over the side. She knew that she had to get moving or she would not make it down the treacherous mountain trail before the sun set, and yet she felt such a glow that she felt that somehow God would light the way for her if she tarried. She finally decided to pull on her boots and take advantage of the rustic toilet facilities before she started on the road back to civilization. She realized that she was putting off returning to civilization and she thought this is how Moses must have felt when he had to descend from Mt Sinai. And yet, return she must. Those words kept ringing in her head and she pulled her boots from the floor of the back seat.

"Honor and protect my creation.

Recognize and celebrate the diversity I birthed from my womb.

Return my church to the prophets and the mystics."

As she went to brush off her feet before pulling on her socks and boots, she realized that, strangely, her feet were not cut, not even dusty, though she had walked across the rough stones and ashy dirt. They probably should be scratched and perhaps even bleeding, but they were as smooth as the trunk of the Matriarch had been. She pulled on her socks and then her boots, took one last, longing look at the Matriarch and started down the winding dirt road.

Leslie was filled with a sense of elation as well as trepidation as she made the drive down the mountain. She knew she would just barely make it before the sun set. But her fear was not of making that dangerous drive; it was of what lay before her. She realized that she would have to call the magazine and tell them she couldn't write this article. This was not something she would write about, at least not in a travel magazine, and she doubted she could ever put this experience down on paper. She wasn't even sure who to tell or how she would tell anyone, but she knew she would have to tell George. However, she knew even that phone call would be days, maybe weeks, away. She had to digest this all herself first. She had to try to sort out her feelings and then, using her intellect, figure out what her next step was, before she could tell even George. She suddenly had a great urge to be back at home and riding Mancha. She somehow felt Mancha would understand and would be able to console her and guide her. Silly that she thought a horse could do this, and yet she knew he could. The thought of being home and riding Mancha compelled her to want to drive faster, and yet she knew she couldn't increase her speed on this treacherous road. It would be one very long drive back, much longer than the drive there had been. She had been on fire with anticipation of seeing the trees and, although that anticipation usually made the drive slower, it actually seemed to Leslie to go quickly. Her heart seemed to be beating too fast and she felt like she had when she used to drink caffeine, when everything was in fast forward.

As she descended the mountain, there was music in her head, music she couldn't stop. It was another song she had heard at George's first Mass, *Veni, Sancti Spiritu*, Come Holy Spirit. She remembered the drums beating as George slowly processed around the cathedral, sprinkling the assembly with holy water with a freshly cut palm frond. It seemed those drums were in her car as she drove and the smell of the incense permeated the air. She wasn't sure why these images of George's ordination were so strong in her head today, but someday, she would tell him about this drive, along with everything else that had happened to her on the mountain. She remembered reading somewhere, maybe it was in the works of Thomas Merton, about the 'mountaintop experience,' but now she really understood what it meant.

PART II

Chapter 9

Somewhere Over Europe

Leslie made one last attempt at closing her eyes and trying to get some rest before the plane landed in Rome. The Italian was now sleeping, his mouth open and a soft snoring sound emanating from him. His breath smelled of the over-abundance of wine. Leslie had a brief recollection of a homeless man she had seen sleeping on the streets of Washington, DC on her last visit there about a year ago. She had flown to Washington to meet George, who had some kind of business at Catholic University and it had been so good for the two of them to get together. But the memory of that homeless man stayed in her mind for a long time. And now, the same smells and the same sounds were coming from this Italian with his $3,000 suit and $800 Gucci loafers. Leslie thought that she would have preferred sitting next to the homeless man right now. She remembered the look in that homeless man's beautiful green eyes when he opened them after she stopped to give him a dollar. She thought she would just leave the money in the ragged wool cap he held in his lap and go on her way, but then he opened his eyes and smiled. She thought at the time that she had never seen such beautiful eyes, and there was look of sincerity and thankfulness for the smile Leslie had given him along with the twenty-dollar bill she now chose to place in his hand. She didn't usually give handouts to the homeless, but somehow this man seemed different. Even before he opened those magnificent eyes and flashed that open, engaging smile, there was something about him that was different than the homeless men from whom she usually averted her eyes as she walked by. She somehow felt this man would use the $20 to get a hot meal, and maybe even lift himself up from the gutter because of her encouragement. She thought for a minute that this man might be Christ Himself, his eyes were so compelling. To this day, she still wondered about that.

Maybe if the Italian in the next seat had green eyes, she might have been more tolerant of his advances. But these two black coals set in a face with olive-toned skin, reminded her of the shifty eyes of the movie gangsters in the late-night movies. At least he was sleeping now and neither his thoughts nor his words intruded on her reverie. But the soft whisperings of the couple behind her seemed like shouting to Leslie. The two were arguing, quietly, so as not to be overheard. But Leslie heard every word they said and many more unspoken thoughts, like daggers piercing her skull. He hadn't wanted to come on this trip; he was worried about his business back in Long Island. She was already complaining because she knew he would be spending too much time in the business center of their hotel and not shopping with her. She needed a whole new wardrobe because she had gained thirty pounds. He was chiding her about her weight gain; she was blaming him for not spending enough time at home, causing her to drown her sorrows in rich food. Leslie wished she could drown out these voices, these thoughts, but they were all around her. These two were no different than the many others she had heard recently, the lack of confidence in their own abilities and the reality of their inadequacies causing them to find all the weaknesses in each other. So many souls suffering with the same malady, it was just too much for Leslie to bear. The only time she could get away from it all was when she was riding Mancha through the northern Nevada trails, or when she was climbing a mountain trail by herself, miles from civilization.

She thought now about that fateful day six months ago, although this thing was one she knew had been growing in her from the time she was young, maybe from birth. She had always had an uncanny sense of knowing what other people were thinking and feeling, and had a gift for understanding people's motivations and emotions. This gift she sometimes viewed as a curse because it seemed everyone wanted to share their inmost feelings and thoughts with her. And they all expected her to give them advice, or at the very least, to listen to them. It didn't seem to matter if they were young or old, male or female, rich or poor; they all seemed to think Leslie was their psychotherapist, their counselor, or their confessor. This "gift" may be one of the reasons Leslie was attracted to life in rural Nevada, where she found that people seemed to live their own lives, not interfering with other people's lives as had her friends back east. And, of course, she filled many hours by herself—riding, hiking, caring for her animals, or driving around the state visiting interesting little towns like Goldfield, Crystal and Ely. And revisiting all the places she and Michael had enjoyed so much— Virginia City, Truckee, and the Black Rock Desert. It was on the last of these trips that she came to know what her destiny was, at last.

Chapter 10

Rome

George, as always, arose early, went for a brisk walk through St. Peter's Square before dawn, and then settled back in his study with his breviary for his morning prayers before breakfast. George's breakfast was the same every morning, oatmeal with raisins and brown sugar, a sliced tomato and a strong cup of decaffeinated green tea sweetened with raw sugar. Leslie's health-conscious nature was one of the few things the two of them had in common. He sometimes thought that Leslie's goal was to live forever. And if any human could achieve immortality, he thought Leslie would be the one to do it. As for him, the events of the past few months had left him physically drained, although spiritually refreshed. And now, this thing with Leslie would place an added burden on him. Of this he was certain. At the same time, he felt a renewed spirit rising within himself. He knew, however, that what he had only heard from Leslie was only the tip of the iceberg.

This morning, George's walk was not as invigorating as usual. Like Leslie, he was apprehensive and yet excited about their meeting later tonight. He knew Leslie would be in no mood for conversation after her long journey, and he had spent enough mornings growing up with Leslie to know that you didn't want to attempt conversation with her when she was in a foul mood, especially about something this important. And he knew Leslie was always in a foul mood when she didn't have enough rest, something she wouldn't get on the long flight from Reno to New York and then to Rome. So, he had resolved that he would not see her until she had had an opportunity to settle in to her hotel, sleep most of the day and then have a hot shower before they met for dinner. Although it was killing him not to meet her at the airport and start questioning her right away, he let his better judgment win out and sent a driver for her instead. He knew she would prefer it that way.

George was accustomed to deferring to his sister. Even though she was the younger of the two, he always knew she was superior intellectually, and even spiritually, to him. All through school, while he studied long hours to achieve top honors, Leslie managed to maintain even higher grades than he during their eight years at St. Monica's, at Sacred Heart High School, and even throughout most of her college years. The only semester Leslie didn't maintain her grades was the one that she spent on the archeological dig in New Mexico. Leslie was too distracted by the local Native Americans and trying to understand their culture, to really focus on her schoolwork. George actually feared she would fall in love with a handsome, black-haired Indian boy, and not come home at all. But even this temporary slump in her grades was not enough to keep her from graduating magna cum laude, while he himself worked into the wee hours of the morning in order to wear the gold cords of a cum laude graduate.

George sometimes got frustrated with Leslie for always following her heart and not her head. She was so much like their father Henry that it sometimes scared George, because he thought she too would die of a broken heart after Michael's early demise. Even he was surprised, although not as much as everyone else, including her own children, when Leslie announced she was leaving Connecticut and moving to a small ranch near Carson City, Nevada.

George always knew that there was something very special about Leslie, even as a young child. Some, like their grandmother, called her headstrong and stubborn, but George knew that it was more than that. It was more like Leslie had the answers while the rest of world had questions. Growing up, her tenacity sometimes got her in trouble, but most of the time, she was right in the things she chose to cling to, and just as right in the things of which she easily let go.

George had been especially amused by Leslie's threat of entering the convent after breaking up with her first 'real love.' He couldn't imagine her subjecting herself to the kind of discipline that came with religious life. George, on the other hand, had already been convinced he had a vocation to the priesthood, although he had not spoken of this to anyone in the family. The only person who knew about George's plans to enter the seminary was Father O'Malley, his pastor. George had been an altar boy since he was eight and Father O'Malley had always taken a special interest in him, not in the wrong way, but as an older brother might do. It was evident he saw in George a priest in the making. George knew that he would soon have to share his calling with his parents and with Leslie, but something held him back. It might have been Henry's fear that George would never be able to earn a good salary as a parish priest. Henry saw that the church demanded a lot from its priests and that the rewards were few, at least in the material sense. Although Henry's mother was a devout Catholic and would have been ecstatic if Henry had entered the seminary, Henry knew he would never have the stamina to go through all those years of study, living a life of loneliness and driving a ten-year-old car. Henry's son, on the other hand, seemed made for this kind of life, but Henry had dreams for his son, and those dreams did not include a life of self-denial. Like so many of his generation, Henry wanted his children to have a 'better life' than he had had. Although, again like most people his age, he had no idea what this 'better life' really meant. He did know that he did not want his children to live through a depression as Henry and his generation had. Money, Henry thought, was the one thing that would provide that better life, and George knew his father would be terribly disappointed if he did not enter law school, as Henry and Greta had been planning.

As much as money was a motivator for Henry, George was pretty sure that once his father learned of his decision, he would support him in it. Greta, on the other hand, would never understand his calling to the priesthood. Greta was a convert to Catholicism, and, because of her Protestant ethic, she had to follow through on her promise to Henry and to Father Callahan, who had married them. She would raise her children in the Church, but she never quite understood the whole celibacy thing. She was convinced there was no logical reason at all for the Church to make such demands on its priests. No wonder Martin Luther broke away from the Church! Greta would not feel that pride that the Irish Catholic mothers in their neighborhood felt when announcing they had a son in the seminary, nor would she brag to other women at the market about, "my son the priest." Yes, Greta would take it much harder than Henry. But Leslie would be the hardest one to tell. As much as the two of them shared all their lives, this would be the one thing they couldn't share. Leslie, he knew, already had it planned that they would go to the same university and that George would have scoped out the sororities, the professors and the social life before Leslie arrived as a freshman, so she could jump right into college life. And of course, George would introduce her to all the Big Men on Campus. He would be a junior by the time she arrived, active in the best fraternity and at the top of his class. How could George tell Leslie that he would be going to the seminary, a place where women were taboo, and that from that time on, George would be moving in a world that Leslie could never share. It wasn't that Leslie wouldn't understand church life; she probably spent as much time in church as George did, and was unusually spiritual for a fourteen-year-old girl. But George knew it would crush Leslie to know that he would be entering a world in which she could never participate.

George was surprised at Leslie's response when he told her of his plans, even before talking to their parents. She was thrilled that he had found himself at such an early age. She felt, and George agreed, that she would probably be forty or fifty and still trying to figure out what she wanted to be when she grew up. He couldn't believe her reaction. She was ecstatic for him, proud to think that she would have a brother who was priest, and ready to support him when he told their parents. And of course she was secretly thrilled to be the first person, besides Father O'Malley, to know of George's decision. George did worry, however, for more than a brief minute, that Leslie might try to disguise herself as a man and enter the seminary herself. He kept thinking of that movie where Barbra Streisand tried a similar stunt and succeeded in getting into a conservative rabbinical school. The thought intrigued George and he smiled as he pictured Leslie studying for the priesthood and going to all sorts of lengths not to be found out. He just kept thinking about those childhood days of her wanting to be a cowboy, and it wasn't much of a stretch to think she would transfer that longing into a desire for the priesthood. But of course, that could never work, and they both knew it. Fortunately, the issue was never raised by either of them and as Leslie became more involved with her busy social life and George prepared to enter the seminary, they both knew that they would always share a closeness of spirit even though they would be moving in very different worlds.

George's climb through the hierarchy of the Church moved at a much faster pace than he had ever suspected it would. Shortly after his ordination, he became a pastor of his own church when Father Leary, the aging alcoholic pastor of the small rural New York State parish to which he was first assigned died unexpectedly. The Bishop of Albany, knowing that George was up to the task, appointed him interim pastor, and then, a year later, named him pastor of St Bridgett's. Some of the older priests in the Diocese resented George's move into a full pastorate at such a young age. However, most of the priests in the Diocese respected George for his intelligence, his deep spirituality, and his Irish charm that seemed to work on men and women alike, and especially on the hierarchy of the Church. George was also a good fundraiser, a valued skill in the Bishop's eyes. Bishop O'Hanlon knew that if anyone could get St. Bridgett's out of debt, it would be George. Not only was he a prudent investor, but it seemed that ever since George was assigned to St. Bridgett's, the weekly collections and special collections rose dramatically. The parishioners loved him and opened their wallets as well as their hearts.

After thirteen years of increasingly more demanding assignments, George was stunned when he was approached to become the Bishop of the Diocese of Allentown, Pennsylvania. It was a small Diocese and one with no apparent major challenges, but George was shocked to think he would be named a bishop at such an early age. On the drive to Allentown from Albany, George was filled with trepidation, but also with eagerness to think that he was being considered for this appointment. He met with the current bishop, who was getting ready to retire, in his modest brick residence on Turner Street. Bishop Neal was a jovial man in his seventies, who greeted George at the door himself. He was known to be a man of pure heart who lived simply and who was well liked by most of the priests and virtually all of the people of the Allentown Diocese. George knew it would be hard to fill these shoes. He also knew from his research that the Diocese, although not in crisis, had its share of challenges, particularly the number of small parishes and the number of aging priests, which would soon result in a lack of pastors to fill all those parishes. He was told his first big job would be to close some parishes and parochial schools in the diocese in order to solve the financial crisis that was rapidly reaching unmanageable proportions. George's ability to surround himself with competent advisors, invest money wisely and raise money were much needed by this Diocese, and were the reasons he was chosen for this assignment. Of course, it was well-known that he was also a deeply spiritual priest, well versed in Canon Law and the documents of Vatican II. Although there was a concern that George's liberal thinking and intellectualism might overwhelm the conservative flock of this mostly rural Pennsylvania Diocese, the powers that be understood that his charismatic personality would soon win over the people. Bishop Neal was convinced that George's work to relieve some of the priests of their multiple assignments would be most welcomed, endearing him to the priests of the diocese (and of course, we was relieved that he would not need to deal with closing parishes and making enemies). Bishop Neal, while well liked by the people, had faced much criticism from his priests because of his refusal to consider closing churches or merging schools. He would rather have a priest serve as pastor of four parishes, as some were doing, than to close a parish, which might cause the wrath of the parishioners to fall upon him as Bishop. Although most of the priests liked Neal personally, his inability to make prudent decisions on the closing of churches frustrated the overworked priests to no end. The number of priests on leave of absence for medical and personal reasons was on the rise, and the number of early deaths and the rate of alcoholism among priests were beginning to reach an alarming level. It was time for a new Bishop to come in to shake up the Diocese.

Once George found himself settled into the rolling hills of eastern Pennsylvania in the City of Allentown, he found that there were more challenges than he had anticipated. Bishop Neal's friendly outgoing manner and simple lifestyle had endeared him to his flock, but his administrative skills left much to be desired. There was more debt than George's initial cursory review of the financial statements had indicated. Much of this was due to Neal's refusal to close parishes, many of which had less than a hundred active families. As George reviewed the status of the churches of the diocese, he was amazed to find that, particularly in Schuylkill County, in the northernmost reaches of the diocese, there were towns with six Catholic parishes serving a town of a few thousand people. This disturbing situation had deep-seated roots in the early coal mining days where there were divisions between the mine owners and the mainly Eastern European mine workers. To this day, there were numerous ethnic parishes in the Diocese, especially in Schuylkill County, because years before the Lithuanians refused to share a pew with the Poles, who wouldn't associate with the Italians, who wouldn't worship with the Irish, and on and on. The result was that in many of the small towns, within one block, you could find a Polish parish, an Irish parish, a Slovak parish and an Italian parish. And, with the closing of the coal mines years before, many of the younger people had moved to Lehigh Valley, Berks County or Philadelphia, seeking job opportunities not found in their economically depressed county. As a result, many of the churches were predominantly populated by people over the age of sixty, hardworking and not wealthy, but extremely generous to their churches. Despite their generosity, there was only so much a parish priest could do with a flock of seventy or eighty widows and widowers and a few young families who opted to stick it out in their home town, mainly because of their duty to aging parents. George was amazed at how much some of these local parish priests were able to do considering the circumstances. He found that the priests were tight-fisted with their limited funds, but always responded well to the Bishop's Annual Appeal. They were far more generous than the well-to-do parishes in the larger cities of Bethlehem, Allentown and Reading. Although the total dollars were far higher in the larger city churches, the number of people giving and the per capita gift amount were much higher in the small ethnic parishes.

George much preferred socializing with the priests in the northern reaches of the Diocese. They were totally honest with him, lived simple lives and it was easy to see why they were so well liked by their parishioners. Some of the best memories of his time as Bishop of the Allentown Diocese were those of celebrating the confirmation masses in these simple rural parishes, where the priests usually invited him for a meal of pieroggis and galumpkis in their small, and often gaudily decorated rectories. He much preferred these unpretentious meals to the elaborate repasts some of the younger priests in the large city parishes felt they were obligated to provide for their Bishop. He found the priests and the parish staff entirely too stiff and formal at the confirmations in Reading, Bethlehem and Allentown.

Like his predecessor, George preferred getting behind the wheel of his own car to being driven by a staff member, traveling the roads of the rural areas of his diocese. Some of his deepest prayer experiences were on early morning drives as the sun burned off the fog covering the Gordon Naugle Trail between the two parishes in Minersville and the one in Schuylkill Haven, or on the mountain roads between Shenandoah and Ringtown, dividing coal country from farm land. All in all, George was happy in the Allentown Diocese and the progress he made in closing parishes, merging parochial schools and getting the diocese back in the black again, did not go unnoticed. He was soon assigned a larger diocese in Metuchen, New Jersey, where, after just three years, he had made a name for himself through his knowledge of canon law, his ability to balance a budget and at the same time, share a deep spiritual connection with his people. Before long, he was Archbishop of Boston and shortly after that, one of the youngest Cardinals in the Church, spending most of his time in Rome assuring that the current liberal's Pope John XXIV's agenda was implemented and that the prior Pope Gregory XVII's ultraconservative rulings were reversed.

Most of the world had been shocked when Mbuto Mumbawu was elected Pope. The young Cardinal Mumbawu was outspoken in his criticism of Gregory and called for the Cardinals to protest this Pope's silencing of the liberal theologians, especially those from third world countries who found many of the edicts issued by Rome irrelevant in their homelands where people were starving, dying of AIDS and oppressed by their political leaders. Mumbawu, however, was well liked and respected by most of the Cardinals, many of whom agreed with him but were too afraid to speak out as vehemently as he did. They respected him not only for his courage, but also for his knowledge of scripture. He had spent a lifetime studying ancient texts and was one of the world's foremost scripture scholars. He was convinced that for the Church to survive, it would have to be restored to more closely resemble the Church started by Jesus' apostles, living out Christ's teachings and not bogged down by hierarchy. Mumbawu's election to the papacy was as much of a shock to him as it was to the rest of the world. He was not prepared for this at all; he would have been perfectly content to live out his life studying the Dead Sea Scrolls and the other ancient texts for clues into the direction today's Church should be headed. He was convinced, from his readings of ancient texts, that the early church would have been more relevant today had it followed the Johannine philosophy, rather than the hierarchical structure of the Petrine sect and, at times, he even questioned the validity of the papacy itself for today's Church. However, he embraced his new mission with vigor. He immediately set out to bring about drastic changes, including a new social action agenda, and appointed his friend George Cardinal Castle as the new Cardinal Prefect in charge of the Congregation for the Doctrine of the Faith. And George accepted his new appointment willingly and enthusiastically. He and Mumbawu had spent many hours together talking about the Church they dreamed of restoring to one that more closely resembled the church established by Jesus.

But now, George was facing what might be the most critical challenge of his priesthood. Dealing with his own sister, the one person in his life he could always count on to be truthful with him, and who was now about to shake the very roots of his Church. He believed everything that Leslie had told him in a long, emotion-filled phone conversation, and yet, how could he believe her story, even though he knew that what she shared on the phone was just the beginning of an even more incredible tale? He needed to see her in person, to hold her hand, to see first hand the change in her that he knew was evident in her voice. This would be the longest day of George's life, knowing that Leslie would be just a few blocks from him, resting in the Vatican Hotel until their dinner tonight. He would try to fill the hours while he waited to meet Leslie for dinner with prayer and work, but he couldn't concentrate even on the Taize prayer that had been so much of his spiritual life for years. Yes, this would be a long day!

George had been concerned that he hadn't had a call from Leslie in several months, since that first call when she had told him some of her recent adventure. He had known immediately that there was something different about Leslie, something he would soon learn more about than he might want to know. She normally called him at least once a month, even though they were generally in touch by email weekly. But even her recent emails contained an evasive, almost distant, tone and he wondered if she was okay. He knew he should call her, but things were quite hectic for him right now. Pope John XXIV was off on another trip to Africa, trying to bring together the heads of state to deal with the growing AIDS pandemic and political upheaval. With his friend and mentor gone for a month, George had to deal with the conservative Cardinals who used every absence of the Pope as an opportunity to question this Pope's priorities; after all, he was head of the Church, not a world political leader. Some of the more outspoken critics dared to voice their concerns, "Why doesn't he leave these issues to the World Health Organization and the United Nations?" The conservatives thought he should instead be focused on the growing lack of unity in his own Church. The American Bishops were a troublesome lot, according to the conservatives, always coming up with some new challenge to the Church's tradition. The Americans had romanticized Liberation Theology and Oscar Romero, who foolishly got himself shot back in the 1970's. The conservatives feared that if the Americans and some of the other liberal factions didn't cease and desist their constant political interference, perhaps even the Pope himself would be the target of a terrorist attack. Those crazy political zealots, some of them thought, would attack the Pope for not using his influence to put a stop to this radical political action on the part of some of his Bishops.

Chapter 11

Dissention in Rome

Antonio Cardinal Ferranti, the most painful thorn in George's side, used every absence of John XXIV to drive the wedge between the liberals and the conservatives even deeper. George thought that if the papacy had ever allowed for a process like impeachment, Ferranti would have started impeachment proceedings soon after John XXIV took office. Ferranti was crushed at the election results, and if he could have prevented the white smoke from rising from the Vatican chimney, he would have done so. Ferranti had been a 'Pope in the making' ever since his ordination to the priesthood, maybe even since he was an altar boy at San Segundo's in Palermo. Ferranti grew up on a small Sicilian farm, the second youngest of twelve children. Maria and Nicholas, his parents, were tired by the time Antonio came along—Maria tired of raising children and Nicholas, just tired of living. When Antonio's younger brother, Giuseppe came along, Maria prayed a secret prayer of thanksgiving when the doctor told her she would not have any more children. Giuseppe quickly became the apple of Nicholas' eye and the tiredness that had plagued Nicholas for so many years, seemed to vanish.

Antonio was jealous of his younger brother and became devoted to his duties as an altar boy in an effort to escape watching Nicholas and Maria doting over his younger brother. The older children seemed accustomed to being shunted off every time a new baby came along, and knew they would spend a lot of hours taking care of the newest Ferranti, but Antonio had been the baby for too long, his younger brother arriving just after his fifth birthday. And as Giuseppe grew up, his good looks and winning smile didn't make it any easier for Antonio to accept him. No, Antonio would seek solace somewhere other than in his family's bosom. It was 'Great Mother Church' that would suckle Antonio and would be his source of knowledge. He was intent, from the time of his First Holy Communion, on following the path to holiness through the priesthood. And Monsignore Albreghetti would be his father. Antonio quickly forgot about his barren, loveless home life under the tutelage of Monsignore Albreghetti who was delighted to be able to shape this young man into the kind of priest he knew was needed in the Church. Albreghetti had envisioned the future of the Church as one that was undergoing changes—too many changes—and something had to be done about it. He would teach young Antonio about the true destiny of the Church, to maintain the status quo, to rout the liberals whom he felt were about to take over the Church. And Antonio learned his lessons well. He was sent to the seminary at the age of fourteen, Maria and Nicholas, happy to have one less mouth to feed, and of course proud that they would be celebrities in their village once they had a priest for a son.

Antonio was ordained just two weeks after his twenty-third birthday, after having completed his studies in record time. He did not go home for the summer to help on the farm as most of the other boys did; let Giuseppe get his hands dirty for a change. He stayed and studied canon law with Father Birogni and the history of the Church with Brother Aldi while the other young men were enjoying a holiday with their families even if, for most of them, it involved more farm work than relaxation. He especially enjoyed canon law, partly because he thought Father Birogni was the most intelligent man he had ever known, perhaps the most intelligent in all of Italy, and partly because he knew this would be important knowledge for a Pope to possess. It was clear to Antonio that he would someday be Pope. After all, it was always an Italian and Antonio would be the best priest in Italy.

It wasn't long before Antonio thought his dream would happen. He rose to the office of Bishop in record time, just as George had, and then Cardinal followed in what seemed like just a few years. In fact, Antonio and George were both appointed Cardinals at an age unprecedented in their respective times, although a number of years apart and by two different Popes. Cardinal Ferranti was, in fact, disturbed by George's rise in the Church, perhaps more because George reminded him of the handsome and personable Giuseppe, who was now an actor of all things, than because of George's obvious liberal slant. Antonio and George would come to odds many, many times because of their differences in theology, if not because of their differences in personality. George Castle was handsome and engaging, well liked by most of the other Cardinals, even those who differed with his political and theological viewpoints. But Popes weren't chosen because of their good looks and charisma, the way American presidents were. Antonio was certain that if George had chosen politics instead of the priesthood, the foolish Americans would easily have elected him President, solely on the basis of his charm and good looks. But the Church operated on a different standard. It would be Antonio's devotion to the Church and to Pope Gregory that would be remembered when the time came. Ferranti was devastated when the upstart from Africa was elected Pope, an African Pope indeed! As though the Pole and the German weren't bad enough! And, after all Gregory and he had done to reverse some of the damage done by John XXIII.

Ferranti felt that he and Mumbawu had been enemies from the first time they laid eyes on each other. Mumbawu never said an unkind word about anyone, but Ferranti knew that the man didn't like him. It was the way he went out of his way to avoid Ferranti, and the way the other Cardinals looked at him when in Mumbawu's presence, as though they had some kind of secret that Antonio couldn't share, that convinced Ferranti that there was some kind of holy war going on between the two of them. Although not fought with swords or incendiary devices, it was more like the cold war the Americans and Russian had fought so many years ago. When Pope Gregory became gravely ill, Ferranti was convinced his time was coming. He would soon be Pope, his childhood dream! He became very soft and mellow, treating his brother cardinals with more respect than ever before. He began practicing his words of acceptance over and over in his head, until he had the developed the perfect address for when the vote was taken. He thought there might be some opposition in favor of Cardinal Sergio, from Calabria. He also had been close to Pope Gregory and was more personable than Antonio, but he lacked the expertise in canon law that Ferranti had, a knowledge that far outweighed that of any of the other cardinals. And none of them had written as extensively as Ferranti. Of his contemporaries, only Gregory himself was more published than Ferranti. The first vote was a close one, closer than Ferranti had expected. And he thought that if those silly Americans hadn't been involved in the vote, it would have clearly gone to Ferranti. But there were several votes for Castle and even a few for Mumbawu, the Nigerian. Well, when it came time for the next vote, they surely would realize that those two didn't stand a chance. After all, Castle was one of the newest Cardinals in Rome and Mumbawu was Black, for God's sake! The votes then would be divided between Ferranti and Sergio and Ferranti certainly would have the edge; he had age, experience and intellect on his side plus the personal friendship with the late Pope Gregory. That had to go a long way with the older Cardinals who thought so highly of Gregory. Ferranti could scarcely believe his ears when the final vote was taken—Mumbawu would be Pope! It couldn't be, after all his prayers, his whole life preparing for this moment, and knowing he would not have another opportunity, unless Mumbawu had an untimely death. But Mumbawu was young and vibrant and would likely still be Pope long after Ferranti closed his eyes. And the worst humiliation was that he would have to serve under this African Pope, who was the ultimate liberal; it made Ferranti's blood boil to think about it.

The next few years were the hardest of Ferranti's life, much more challenging than the years he had spent at seminary, even more difficult than the years working from before dawn to after dusk on the farm while Giuseppe prepared for his 'career' as an actor. He had to deal first with the humiliation of being overlooked by his peers although it was clear he was the obvious choice for Pope; then he had to face being replaced as the Pope's closest advisor by Castle, now the right-hand-man of this new Pope, who had added insult to injury by choosing the name John XXIV, making it clear that he would follow in the footsteps of the liberal John XXIII. After all the years Ferranti and Gregory had worked so closely together to reverse the tide of liberalism that followed Vatican II. And just when they were making clear progress, Gregory developed a cancerous stomach, probably due to rich foods and lack of activity. Gregory had always been more interested in work than he was taking care of his physical needs. Once the cancer was diagnosed, it didn't take long before it was rampant in the Pope's body, spreading to just about every organ. Perhaps had he paid more attention to his physicians' advice, he would have lasted long enough to assure that Ferranti would be Pope. Ferranti had never forgiven him for dying before he had used his influence with the cardinals to assure that the Papacy would be in good hands, conservative hands, for years to come. Ferranti was still relatively healthy and would surely have the time to complete the work he and Gregory had started. But, alas, it was not to be.

Chapter 12

Back in the Carson Valley

Once Leslie arrived home from her trip to the Bristlecones, she knew even before she took that long ride on Mancha that she had been changed forever. Mancha sensed the change in her immediately. He was more gentle and calm than he had ever been. If anything, Mancha had always been unpredictable, sometimes to the point that Leslie wasn't even sure he would let her mount. They had always had a special bond that allowed Leslie to know his feelings and when he didn't want her to ride him, she would take out one of the other horses, but those rides always left Leslie with a feeling of regret, like the way she felt when she was fourteen and thought she had lost her one true love and would never recapture that loss. Leslie thought about George's reaction at the loss of her first boyfriend. Even though she was two years younger, she had started dating long before George even thought about inviting a girl out. Vince was a poor choice for Leslie and she soon realized that. Although he was good looking and charming, for a fourteen year old, he also thought that he could tame Leslie and keep her on a tight leash. She soon set him straight on that notion and made it clear that the relationship would be on her terms or not at all. Like most fourteen-year-old boys, Vince couldn't handle that much authority in a female and soon found another girl whom he could mold into his pattern of the ideal 'woman.' Leslie was infuriated by Vince's reaction and stormed around the house for a week swearing to enter the convent and never look at a "stupid boy" again. Of course, Leslie had been wildly popular with the boys, although most of them thought she was a real challenge. George had said that it would take a real Petruchio to tame Leslie and that he certainly couldn't imagine her being tamed by any Mother Superior in a convent.

However, when Leslie found Michael, she knew that the loss of that girlhood love was nothing compared to the joy she felt with Michael. And riding Mancha after one of his 'hissy fits' was almost as rewarding. It seemed so much sweeter after having been denied that pleasure for even a day. Today, Mancha was more than compliant. He was eager to have her on his back, as though he somehow knew Leslie had a special secret to share and he would be the first one to hear it. And indeed, share it she did. For the first two hours, Leslie reflected with Mancha on her childhood and her life with Michael.

Leslie's first recollection of hearing her parents argue was over the limousine business that her father was sure would be their ticket to easy street. Henry had not counted on a driver showing up drunk and wrecking his first limo. Once the insurance claim was settled, the business folded and Henry's next big dream was real estate. He financed this big venture by re-mortgaging the house, causing Greta to threaten divorce. Of course, her fear of the repercussions from the Catholic church would never allow her to think seriously of divorcing Henry, but Greta knew he would be so devastated at the mere thought of losing her, that he would buckle down and try to live up to her expectations.

And it worked. Henry tried his best to be more practical while still pursuing his dream of supporting Greta and the children in a manner that far exceeded the meager life he had had as a child. Things went along pretty smoothly for several years with the real estate dream, until too many tenants who were slow payers and house wreckers put an end to this venture. Then Henry decided to use his natural talent with gadgets to devote all his time to inventing the next big household gadget. After several failed attempts and a small fortune in patent attorney fees, this dream went the way of the limo business and the real estate fiasco.

Leslie still remembered the shock of losing both her parents in such a short time. Greta's diabetes had finally gotten the best of her, and Henry, unable to go on without Greta, died of a broken heart just eleven days after they laid Greta to rest. The doctors said it was a stroke, but Leslie knew that it was just as her mother had always said—the family, especially Henry, couldn't go on without her and Greta had always prayed not to be the first one to go. George, of course, got through the last weeks of Greta's illness and her dying much better than Leslie and her father had. The two of them cried a lot, looked at old photographs for hours on end, questioned God's wisdom and vented their anger at Greta for not taking better care of her health. She just could never give up those sweet desserts although Leslie and George tried so hard to make her stick with her diet. Henry, of course, always gave in, and every Saturday brought her those cream puffs she loved so much from the farmers' market, and overlooked the chocolate Greta kept hidden in the back of the cupboard. It was no surprise to Leslie when Greta's diabetes escalated into numerous other health problems including the liver failure that finally killed her. Henry never really recovered from Greta's passing and had a stroke just ten days later on the day Leslie had planned to leave for home, after staying with him to go through Greta's things. She wasn't sure she could deal with another funeral to plan, more grieving and, of course, more legal details to wade through. Leslie was glad George was there to take care of the funeral arrangements and help settle the estate. She was amazed at how much was involved, even through her parents had little in the way of assets other than the modest three bedroom home in which she and George had grown up. And then, she had to face it all again in what seemed like such a short time.

As she rode, Leslie recalled what had drawn her to Nevada after Michael's death. She remembered her reaction at seeing the mountains with the windswept trees on the first vacation she and Michael took out west. They had read about the Donner party and knew they had to visit that fateful spot. After a flight into Reno, their time there, and the drive to to various points of interest In Nevada and California, was one of the best times the two of them had had together. They spent three weeks traveling in the area, including a trip to Pyramid Lake, seeing the only remaining water from the Great Basin that had once covered the whole western part of the United States. They had enjoyed the nightlife of Reno, "the biggest little city in the world," and Virginia City, filled with gunslingers and wanna be cowboys. They had even visited Las Vegas although Leslie argued that she really wasn't interested in seeing "Sin City." However, once they had arrived in Vegas, she found she was actually quite fascinated with the contrast between the palm trees and the desert landscape. They hiked to see the petroglyphs in the Valley of Fire, 'camped' in the rustic motel by the shores of Lake Mead, saw the bighorn sheep near Hoover Dam and visited Bonnie Springs Ranch (a pretty hokey tourist trap, but at least there were 'cowboys'). She almost thought she had come home. They talked about moving there someday, but Leslie just knew she wouldn't fit in with the botox-ed and siliconed women that filled the hotels and restaurants at which they dined in Las Vegas. The women in Reno were more her type, rugged ranch women, not the tall, skinny blondes who all seemed to wear leather skirts and pointy, open backed shoes that flip-flopped with every step. Leslie could never quite understand today's shoe styles; open backed tennis shoes were the first ones that took Leslie by surprise. What was the point of that? And then when the pointy open backed pumps became the footwear of choice for most women, Leslie became even more adamant about sticking with her sensible shoe styles—cowboy boots, loafers and, when she did have a need to dress up, she chose the sensible 'flight attendant' styles worn by women who spent all day on their feet. No, Las Vegas would just not blend in with Leslie's lifestyle, although living in northern Nevada she could easily drive to some of her favorite Southern Nevada desert hideaways like the Hot Springs in Calienti, Cathedral Gorge, and the only non-gaming city in Nevada, Boulder City, whenever she wanted. Although the Reno area was where she felt most at home, she remembered every mile of that trip with Michael fondly and decided that there wasn't a single part of Nevada that she didn't love.

Both she and Michael had been fascinated by the rough terrain and the forbidding mountains, and wondered how the pioneers who crossed those mountains had the will and determination to attempt that crossing. She was filled with trepidation on some of those mountainous roads without guardrails, driving their rental car, an air-conditioned, finely balanced SUV.

Although most of her family and friends, including her best friend Sara, were convinced that this move to Nevada was a rash decision, one that Leslie would soon come to regret, and that she would be packing her bags to head home within six months, Leslie knew that this would be her home forever. Once she had picked out a small ranch near Carson City, it didn't take her long to complete the move. She had sold the house in Connecticut to daughter Valerie and her husband, Gary, who were expecting another baby and would need the four-bedroom home. And since she and Valerie shared the same taste when it came to interior decorating, she had left most of the family heirloom furniture there for Valerie and her family. She even gave most of her clothing to Valerie, who wore the same size. Although she was a good four inches shorter than Valerie, Leslie's skirts would be fine for Valerie since she could wear hers much shorter than Leslie would ever dare to. She wouldn't need most of her city clothes on the ranch. She lovingly packed her books, photos and a few items of clothing, including her favorite Irish cable knit sweater that Michael had bought her on one of their trips to Ireland, along with the handsome secretary and the hope chest that had belonged to her grandmother Petra and she and Andre set out to drive across the country with a small U-Haul truck carrying the only physical possessions that meant anything to Leslie, now that Michael was gone.

After two hours of reflecting on her past, Leslie talked in a hushed voice to Mancha, telling him the whole story of her experience on the mountaintop. She seemed especially reverent when she talked about Petra's horseback riding and about her Tlingit and Paiute ancestors who were skilled horsewomen. She told Mancha about Pyramid Lake, how she felt when she and Michael had first experienced the lake, and about the tribe, once led by one of her female ancestors, who guarded the Pyramid for so many years and still lived in its shadow, both literally and figuratively. She shared with Mancha her experience of the Creation and her fear and trepidation as she drove down that mountainous road. Although she still had that nagging fear lurking somewhere in her soul, she was also filled with a peace she had never experienced before and a joy that filled her so completely. She was almost afraid to let anyone see her lest her outward transfiguration, reflecting her internal experience, would frighten people. In fact, since she had come down that mountain, she had made it a point to avoid people. She went to drive-through windows in fast food restaurants to get a salad and tea, sent her ranch hand for groceries and stopped to pick up her mail in her post office box long after she knew the post office windows would be closed just so she wouldn't have to face another human being. She was afraid that if anyone asked her about the outward change which she was sure must be apparent, she might just blurt out the whole truth and if she did, they might send her to a hospital for the insane. She knew she would indeed have to face people sooner or later, but she had to commune with nature and with Mancha first.

She and Mancha finally set out on her favorite trail, one that went through the woods and by the Truckee River towards Fallon. They stopped at the river for Mancha to drink and for Leslie to wash her face in the cleansing water. From the backpack she carried, Leslie pulled out some carrots she would share with Mancha, an apple, a bottle of ice cold spring water (she always had a few bottles half filled and frozen in her freezer), and a handful of almonds for herself, along with her journal. She let Mancha rest for a half hour while she recorded this trip, her overflowing thoughts, and Mancha's 'answers' in her journal. She knew Mancha couldn't really talk, although she sometimes wished he would suddenly become Mr. Ed, a show she had always thought a bit silly. But now she would give anything if Mancha could truly give her the answers she sought. However, she knew he did understand what had happened to Leslie and just knowing this somehow seemed to give her the answers she was looking for. She was beginning to have a sense of the task ahead of her, but she knew it would take her a while to prepare herself to face everyone with this decision. After her four-hour ride with Mancha, she knew she could now face people. She knew she had to do it!

It turned out that she had a rather commonplace first experience with humanity on her calendar, her annual mammogram appointment at High Desert Radiology, the very next morning. Well, if anything could humble a person, having your breast squeezed by a cold metal machine while dressed in an open-front hospital gown and holding your breath, surely could. The appointment went without incident except that Leslie had a strange sensation of being able to read the thoughts of the technician while she went about her work. The technician was thinking about the fight she had just had with her boyfriend the night before. Leslie somehow sensed that the technician thought he dated her just because he knew she examined breasts all day. There was something strange about a man who was so fascinated by what she thought when she looked at other women's breasts all day. Leslie felt the technician's dismay at his unnatural interest in her work, and could 'hear' the fight they had over this issue last evening after dinner. He seemed to think there was something strange about her because of her work, and this strangeness seemed to pique his interests in a rather abnormal way, the technician thought. He really blew his stack when she said it wasn't any stranger than grown men patting each other on the behind during sporting events, and God only knows what went on in those locker rooms. He said that was different and the technician, like Leslie, thought it was high time for men to stop having different standards for their own behavior than they had for women's.

Fearing that she might 'hear' more of such disturbing thoughts from the other women in the office, Leslie tried hard to concentrate on the soft classical music playing in the office as she dressed, paid her bill and walked to the parking lot. The blooms on the purple sage growing by the sidewalk seemed to have become even fuller while she was suffering through this ordeal, and even seemed brighter in color. It must have been a trick of the morning sunlight, or maybe Leslie just hadn't paid as much attention on her way into the office, pulling into the parking lot just about a minute before her scheduled appointment. Leslie had always hated being late and wanted to get inside to check in before someone with a later appointment signed the book before her. Not that the clerks behind the desk really cared, but it was a matter of principle for Leslie to always be on time for appointments, one of the few things she had in common with Greta. Not only did the blooms appear fuller and brighter, but also the entire day seemed to have clarity that was a bit scary. Maybe Leslie's eyes were somehow getting better and she didn't need the glasses she wore any longer. That would certainly be a welcomed treat. She had always hated glasses and she had heard that sometimes people's eyesight actually improved as they aged.

Just as Leslie was musing about the possibility of giving up her glasses, another strange thing happened. There were suddenly a host of beautifully-colored butterflies flying around her, following her to the car. How would she get in the door without slaming the door on any of these magnificent creatures, and if they did get into the car, what if they flew in front of the windshield while she was driving? She had a sudden recollection of the time she had driven home with a car filled with balloons for one of the children's birthday parties, balloons of all colors and sizes. The balloons somehow got loose and kept bouncing around the inside of her station wagon. Although she was afraid then of having the balloons impede her driving vision, she had to giggle at the thought of how she must look, driving down the street with a car full of bouncing balloons surrounding her. She was glad it was just a few short blocks home; then she had to wrestle with the balloons to get them all captured before she opened the car doors. Michael happened to be looking out the front window as she pulled up and laughed hysterically at the sight of Leslie rounding up her renegade balloons. He would be laughing with her now as she envisioned the ten-mile drive home surrounded by brilliantly colored butterflies darting in front of her and landing on the dashboard. Several of the butterflies had actually landed on her arms and she hoped that no one had noticed this phenomenon. Maybe she should run to her car, but that would draw even more attention. She finally decided to just pretend they weren't there at all and she strolled leisurely to her car. As she opened the door, most of the butterflies flew toward the bushes; only the ones on her arms got into the car with her. Leslie was relieved to find that none of them had gotten trapped in the door when she closed it; she was concerned that she might crush some of them between the car and the door when she closed it. She opened the front window of the X Terra and once she had picked up speed, the remaining butterflies flew out the window.

As she drove home, pondering the meaning of this strange phenomenon, she noticed that there seemed to be a lot of birds flying close to her car today. The butterflies had been a gentle invasion, but birds could be nasty and she hoped they didn't swarm towards her car when she pulled into her driveway as the butterflies had in the parking lot. She drove faster in an effort to evade them and eventually she saw them in her rear view mirror soaring towards the sky.

When Leslie arrived home, she made herself a cup of tea and sat looking out the window towards the stables for a long time. What on earth was happening to her? She knew it was all related to her fateful drive to the Bristlecones and her encounter with the Matriarch. Had she really entered the tree itself? Had she really witnessed creation? And what was she supposed to do with the knowledge she had gained there, Those three phrases kept running through her mind—"Honor and protect My Creation; Recognize and celebrate the Diversity I birthed from My Womb; Return My Church to the Prophets and Mystics." What did it all mean and what was Leslie destined to do with this revelation? She thought that she best understood honoring and protecting God's creation. She had always been sensitive to the earth and all that it held. The butterflies, for instance—she would not want to have been responsible for harming a single one of them and was so relieved that they all survived their encounter with her.

She remembered visiting the shoe museum in Toronto once and seeing shoes that the ancient Chinese had worn. The shoes were metal, thong-like inventions that rested on little stilt-like appendages, thereby allowing the wearer to tread as lightly as possible on the earth in order to protect any creatures that might be underfoot. At the time, she had thought it was a bit extreme, but now she held a special reverence for the people who had thought so highly of creation that they designed this unique footwear. She was a member of the Sierra Club and The Nature Conservancy and had donated a portion of all her writing fees and royalties to the Tahoe Rim Trail Association and Keep Truckee Beautiful. Although Leslie knew that there were a number of organizations and government agencies deigned to protect the environment, she knew there was more to be done. But—what?

Diversity was also another issue she felt that she understood pretty well. In her college days, she had marched with Blacks in Alabama and spent that semester with the Native Americans in New Mexico. She was sensitive to the issues of women, gays, and Hispanics and she and Michael had worked for social justice at every level. And yet, again, she knew she was somehow being asked to do more.

The one that really puzzled her was, "Return My Church to the Prophets and Mystics." What did it mean and what could Leslie possibly do about it? This was undoubtedly a question for George, but she knew she was not yet ready to talk with George or anyone else about her experiences and these strange messages. She had to sort it out as best she could for herself first.

As Leslie searched the depths of her soul over those next few weeks, a plan began to emerge in the back of her mind. She became aware of the fact that she had heard those words before—"Honor and protect My Creation"—or at least the thought behind them. She had heard or thought them a long time ago in her own head. It was actually watching a TV commercial, of all things, which birthed this thought. She couldn't recall now who had sponsored that commercial, but she thought it was some department of the United States government. It featured a Native American, the archetypical image of the Old West. This revered symbol of America was watching citizens carelessly discarding their trash on the streets, polluting water, and filling the air we breathe with smoke. The Native American did not say a word but looked on silently as a tear slowly emerged from his saddened eyes and traced its way down that beautiful, weathered face. She remembered thinking at the time that the message of this one lonely tear was "honor and protect my creation." Leslie had always had a special affinity for Native Americans and had always felt that somehow she had Native American ancestors, although she knew intellectually that couldn't be possible since her ancestors had immigrated to the United States from Germany. And yet, there had always been that haunting feeling in her spirit that she had walked this land before, that the sprit of the Native American lived in her. Until her trip to the Ancient Bristlecone Forest, she couldn't imagine how this could be, and yet, she had always known it in her heart to be true. Like most Americans, maybe most of the world, she had always assumed that the migration of humanity across the land that once connected Asia to what is now the state of Alaska had always been one-way traffic. Her encounter with the Matriarch had taught her differently, and she now knew that she did indeed have Native American ancestors.

She had learned on her internship in New Mexico that one of the reasons she had been so attached to Native American culture was their love for the earth and all of creation. She felt the Native Americans revered God's creation perhaps more than any other people before or after them. While she had been in New Mexico, she saw this love of the land slowly coming back to the Native American culture. Like most Americans, the Native Americans children of the fifties had adopted the 'me generation' attitude. However, during the sixties and seventies, in light of the awareness of what pollution and consumerism were doing to our world, she saw a new interest in honoring and protecting the earth. She was intrigued by the young Native American girls who were begging their grandmothers and great grandmothers to show them how to gather the herbs that cured so many of the illnesses the White Man had brought to their nation. Leslie was particularly interested in learning these ancient remedies, because she recalled her own grandmother's expertise and wished then that she had spent more time learning these cures and preventative measures from her own grandmother. So she quickly learned, along with the young women, the secrets of herbal remedies taught by the Navajo ancients. She learned to brew the teas and make the poultices that these women used to protect their families from the evil spirits, which they now understood to be germs and viruses, and she learned from the men how to live off the land and eat only what Nature provided. Those few months among the Navajos in New Mexico was one of the happiest times in her life until, of course, she met Michael.

Now, Leslie realized what she had to do, and a plan, perhaps a totally insane idea, was hatched. She needed to talk to the elders of the Native American tribes, the ones who were now leaders of their people, the ones who, for the first time in their history, had spendable cash and lots of it. Although Leslie was not much of a gambler, she remembered being astounded and delighted when the first Native American casino opened not far from their home in Connecticut. She thought it was perfect payback for all the land the white people had stolen from the Native Americans. They were now going to get rich on the habits of the white people, whose greed was finally working in favor of the people whom they had robbed of everything precious to them, their land, and their honor. And rich they grew, indeed. She had visited the beautiful museum built by the Pequots near the Foxwoods Casino and was amazed at the structure and all it contained. She and Michael had spent hours there one afternoon, enthralled with the fact that the Pequots had used the profits of their casino to fund a monument to their culture. The life-sized models in that museum were of the highest quality, so realistic that you could almost see the eyelashes flutter and the blood flowing through the veins in the arms of the young native men. She had read about the multi-million dollar wonder and wanted to see it first hand, so she and Michael drive down one Sunday after church, spent about an hour looking around the casino, dropped twenty dollars in the slot machines, had a quick lunch and then moved on to the museum, which was the real purpose of their trip. Somehow, Leslie didn't mind spending money in this casino knowing it was going to a good cause.

She recalled a couple of years ago when she and Michael had driven to Atlantic City for the weekend just to see the change in that city after gambling took over. She remembered thinking that the change was certainly not a good one. The wonderful sights and smells she had remembered from her early childhood days visiting the Jersey Shore were gone, replaced by pawnshops, slums, and homeless people. She couldn't help thinking that gaming had ruined this quaint little shore town and she was pleased to see that here it was actually providing a great community asset.

With the beginnings of her plan in her head, Leslie set out to do some research. She found that there were hundreds of Native American casinos and that they were in almost every state in the country. She had had no idea there were so many. She spent weeks researching who owned these casinos, found who the real decision makers were, what their gross revenues were, and what charitable organizations they were supporting. She devised a plan that was actually quite simple, so simple it might not be taken seriously, but she believed in her heart it would work. She then developed a detailed business plan, showing the costs and benefits to the casinos and the tribes that operated them. She knew she would have to find a strong leader, an ally who could help her sell her plan to the others, so she went back to researching and found that her very own Connecticut was the place to start. The Pequot leaders who founded Foxwoods were looked upon as leaders in the gaming industry among Native Americans. She was delighted to hear this because she was pretty sure she could pull some strings to get a meeting with Joseph Runningwater, the wizard behind the curtain that was Foxwoods. She decided to contact her and Michael's old friend, Fred Simms, a high level executive in the gaming commission to see if he could get her an appointment.

Fred was happy to hear from Leslie. He hadn't talked to her since the farewell party her children had thrown when she left for Nevada. Fred was one of the many people who thought Leslie was a bit off her rocker to even think about this move. He was convinced, along with many others, that she would be high-tailing it back to Connecticut within a few months, and was surprised when Leslie's Christmas card arrived each year from Nevada. Knowing Leslie was not much of a gambler, he couldn't imagine her living in Nevada. Of course, Fred's view of Nevada was not unlike that of most East Coast people—that it was gaming country, and other than Las Vegas and Reno, there probably wasn't anything worthwhile in the whole state. If you wanted to gamble, get married or watch a good boxing match, Nevada was your place. But Leslie was accustomed to culture. She would not last long if she couldn't attend the symphony, see a good play or enjoy a high quality museum. Fred couldn't imagine why Leslie would want to meet with Joseph Runningwater; certainly it couldn't have anything to do with the casino unless Leslie had gotten hooked on gambling, which Fred could not imagine. It was probably the museum or one of her charitable interests that prompted this call. Of course, Fred would be able to get her an appointment; it was the least he could do for the wife of his old golfing buddy. Fred had been shocked at Michael's death, and saddened, not just because he would be losing a golf partner, but because he had really valued Michael's friendship and had always admired Michael and Leslie as a couple who inspired greatness in their children and in their friends. Fred had often wished he and Sally had whatever quality it was that made Michael and Leslie such a special couple. Perhaps Sally would still be married to him if they had had this secret, instead of living in Vermont with that shyster lawyer.

Hearing Leslie's voice brought back memories of happier times when the two couples had spent time together, enjoying a great dinner in one of their homes, skiing in Vermont, or working at church carnivals. Once Sally had left Fred, though, things changed. It was probably Fred who felt like the proverbial 'fifth wheel' more than the fact that Michael and Leslie felt uncomfortable around a suddenly-single Fred. Or maybe it was Michael who felt threatened by Fred, now available and still young and handsome, in a bookish sort of way. Did Michael resent the admiration for Leslie that Fred had never tried to hide? After Michael's accident though, Fred felt awkward around Leslie. Maybe it was because she seemed so stunned by Michael's death and he just didn't know what to say to her to comfort her, or maybe he really did have feelings for Leslie that would not be appropriate to share with her now. And so, other than the few minutes in the hallway while she was saying a private goodbye to each of the guests at her farewell party, Fred had not really spoken to her except in the company of others, until now.

Leslie didn't go into great details about her plan, but she did tell Fred enough to pique his curiosity about Leslie's plan to visit Joseph Runningwater. Perhaps the old saying about absence making the heart grow fonder was true, or perhaps it was just that a decent amount of time had passed since Michael's death and his and Sally's divorce that emboldened Fred to invite Leslie to dinner while she was in Connecticut. And he was secretly thrilled at her response. She would love to have dinner with him and share the details of her meeting with Runningwater. And so the plan was put into motion. Fred would call Runningwater first thing Monday morning and was sure he could get her an appointment within two or three weeks. Leslie would check on airfares to Bradley and Providence and let him know how long she would stay once he got her the appointment.

Leslie hesitated about the dinner and even more so about flying into Bradley for this appointment. She certainly could not make a trip to Connecticut and not see her children, and yet, she wasn't sure if she was ready to face them yet. Valerie had already an inkling that something was going on, just from the sound of Leslie's voice when they talked by phone. She had tried to keep correspondence with her children to emails ever since her experience with the Matriarch, because she feared her voice would tremble and give her away. But Valerie, the persistent and intuitive one, would not let two weeks go by without speaking to her mother by phone. Leslie had tried to put off Valerie and Alex as much as possible and thank God, Andre was so busy with his studies at the seminary that he didn't have much time to talk anyway. She knew that it would hard to keep this thing from Andre; he would surely be able to read her like a book. Now she had to decide whether she should fly into Providence, meet with Joseph Runningwater, have dinner with Fred and then head back home on an early morning flight, or try to spend some time with Valerie and Alex in Hartford. As much as she wanted to see them, she knew she couldn't explain all this to them just yet. However, she could tell them about her trip to the bristlecones, leaving out the details, but letting them know that it inspired her to do something to protect the environment, and she could surely tell them about her visit with Joseph Runningwater. Yes, that is exactly what she would do, she resolved.

Monday afternoon found Leslie preparing for her trip. Fred had called at 6:30 that morning, forgetting about the three-hour time difference. After his profuse apology, Leslie assured him it was no problem. As was her habit, she had risen at five, gone for a thirty-minute walk, fed the horses and was now in the kitchen making her oatmeal and brewing green tea when the phone rang. The appointment at Foxwoods was scheduled for two weeks from tomorrow. Leslie would fly into Bradley on Monday, stay with Valerie that evening and then Fred would pick her up Tuesday morning for the drive to Mashantucket. After the meeting and an early dinner, Fred would drop her off at Valerie's for the evening. The next day, Valerie and Alex would both take the day off to spend with their mother. Valerie was concerned about Leslie, knowing there was something very different about her. She thought perhaps there was a man in Leslie's life and Valerie was not happy about the prospect of her father being replaced by some Nevada cowboy. After Leslie's call to arrange the trip, Valerie was even more confounded. What on earth was her mother planning to do at Foxwoods and how did Fred Simms get into the picture; could he the man in Leslie's life? Valerie had always suspected that Fred had a special attraction to Leslie, even when they were both married. Fred was a nice enough guy, but Valerie certainly didn't think Leslie was ready to take a big step like letting another man into her life. She had almost been relieved when she learned that Leslie was spending so much time with her horses. At least she wasn't out dating some man who might prey on Leslie's loneliness.

Valerie was pleased that Alex, upon hearing of his mother's trip, was able to arrange his schedule so that the three of them could spend the day together on Wednesday after Leslie's trip to Foxwoods and before she flew back to Nevada on Thursday morning. She wished they would have more time together, but she knew Leslie wouldn't leave her horses alone too long. Although she had her trusted ranch hand that would feed them for her, she never liked being gone for longer than about four days at a time. Alex, far less suspicious than Valerie, and seemingly not as concerned about Leslie's sudden reconnection with Fred Simms, assured Valerie that their mother was probably involved in some charitable work, possibly something relating to horses, and suspected that her trip to Connecticut would involve asking for a contribution from the Mashantucket Pequots who ran the Foxwoods Casino. Fred, working for the gaming commission, would be Leslie's natural contact into this world, and if anything, Leslie always knew how to make the right connections when she wanted to accomplish something. Alex had always been amazed at his mother's uncanny ability to network her way into anything she wanted. She wasn't in Nevada more than a few weeks when she had landed the job writing for the AAA magazine, found the best place in Nevada to buy horses, hired a trustworthy ranch hand and found a church that perfectly suited her needs. All of this Alex credited to Leslie's networking abilities. And he was sure that she would know just how to get an appointment with a potential funder for her favorite cause. Leslie was a tireless fundraiser when it came to a cause she really cared about. Alex recalled that she had always had a soft spot for animals, especially horses, and now that she was in Nevada, her horses seemed to occupy most of her time. He assured Valerie that there was probably nothing to worry about. Yes, he did agree that the move west had drastically changed his mother, but he felt it was a good change. She was more relaxed now, more inclined to take time for herself, something she had never done enough of before her move to Nevada.

Alex quickly rearranged his schedule when Leslie called to tell him she was coming to Hartford. He would pick her and Valerie up in his new BMW and they would attend mass at St. Thomas's and then head out for breakfast. He knew Leslie always liked to start her day with God and with a healthy, but hearty, breakfast. After breakfast, they would go back to Valerie's and hear about her trip to Foxwoods and about her dinner with Fred Simms. Valerie would have stocked up on Leslie's favorite fruits and organic salad fixings and would make a light lunch for them all on the patio. They might even take a brief swim after lunch in the heated pool Valerie enjoyed so much. Although there were a lot of friends Leslie would love to see while she was in town, this was definitely a family day and Leslie would be looking forward to seeing her grandchildren that evening at their big family dinner. They had spent many hours sharing good food, good coffee, and good wine around the long dining room table that Leslie had left in the house for Valerie, but somehow Alex suspected this family meal would be different from all those past dinners. If Valerie's suspicions were correct, their mother had big news to tell them and would share her adventures in the West with that special dramatic flair only she could pull off. Alex wished Andre could be here, but it was soon time for his final exams and he knew Andre couldn't leave the seminary now. Andre planned to go visit Leslie as soon as the semester ended in a few weeks and he would hear Leslie's story then.

The two weeks before her trip went by quickly, because Leslie was busy preparing her presentation for Joseph Runningwater and making final arrangements for the work that needed to be done around the ranch. Before she knew it, it was time to pack and she wanted to make sure she had just the right outfit for her meeting at Foxwoods. She wanted to look professional but yet down to earth. She wanted Runningwater to be able to identify with her. Although she couldn't tell him her whole story, she wanted to clearly convey her Native American roots. She finally selected a pair of khaki twill pants, her low cowboy style boots, a soft leather, wine colored blazer and western style, dressy shirt that picked up the khaki and burgundy colors of her outfit. Perhaps not suitable attire for dinner with Fred, but the meeting with Runningwater was of utmost importance to Leslie and would set the pace for her wardrobe for the four days of the trip. For Wednesday with the family, she would wear jeans with a soft pink cashmere sweater, and the leather blazer for the morning out. She would travel to Connecticut in the same jeans and wear the twill khakis on the flight home. Leslie was a firm believer in packing light, so the one pair of boots would be her footwear for the entire trip. Wearing the jeans and blazer on the flight Monday with a white turtleneck, she would only need to pack the khakis and two tops. This, along with her underwear, pajamas and slippers, and her limited toiletries would easily fit in a small overnight bag she could carry on the plane. The material she had prepared for Runningwater and her special food supply for the long flight would fit in the leather tote bag she always carried. In her tote bag she always had a supply of tea bags, Stevia natural sweetener, packaged tuna, some napkins, forks and spoons, and some almonds and dates. She just needed to add her fresh foods that morning, apples, carrots and celery, and she would be ready to go.

That morning she rose early to take a short ride on Pedro, leaving Mancha behind. She knew if she took him out, she would lose track of time and not make her flight. She asked Manuel, the ranch hand, who normally came in three days a week, to drive her to the airport so he could use the X Terra while she was away in case he needed to pick up supplies. Manuel would be coming in every day while she was away to take care of the horses and do some repairs that had been piling up over the unusually cold winter. On the drive to Reno, they went through the list of things to be done while she was away, one last time. Manuel was a hard worker and a personable young man, but he sometimes needed prompting to get everything done. Although Leslie usually welcomed their little chats over her tea and Manuel's strong black coffee (a habit she had tried to break him of, warning him of the dangers of caffeine), she sometimes found that he had frittered away the day chatting with her instead of getting all his chores done. It wasn't that he asked to be paid for this time. If anything, he underreported his hours every two weeks. Leslie suspected that he felt a little sorry for her, trying to run a ranch all by herself, and thought she couldn't really afford him. However, she also thought he probably needed the company more than he needed the money. He had simple tastes and didn't even own a car; he usually walked or rode his horse, Black Jack, everywhere he went. Occasionally he would ride to Reno with Leslie in her X Terra, especially when they needed to shop for things they needed for the ranch. On these trips, Leslie knew he hit the casinos and played a little poker, his one vice, but she didn't complain. It gave her time to visit the museum or the library.

Once she had boarded the plane in Reno, she could only relax for a short time, before she had to transfer in Las Vegas for Bradley. She was glad Southwest had added this new flight to their schedule. It made it so much easier to transfer in Las Vegas instead of stopping somewhere in the Midwest as she had to do on previous trips. Once the flight left Vegas, however, she could kick off her shoes, order a cup of hot water to brew some organic caffeine-free, green tea and review her proposal to the Pequots. Once she felt she had her presentation down pat, she put the folder away, opened her tote bag and pulled out the three books she had brought along, one on the gaming industry written by a Las Vegas journalist who had studied the industry from Nevada's early frontier days to modern-day online gambling, another on the ecological disaster awaiting our world, and the third a history of the Pequots. She wanted to be prepared for anything Runningwater might throw at her during this meeting. Leslie spent the rest of the trip studying the parts of each of these books she thought would be most pertinent for her meeting.

Chapter 13

Connecticut

As the plane was landing at Bradley, a thought occurred to Leslie—this trip might actually help fulfill two of the edicts she had received on the mountaintop—"Honor and protect My Creation" and "Recognize and celebrate the Diversity I birthed from My Womb." Perhaps it was the diverse populations of this world who would save it from destruction. The Native American population was certainly the place to start, but perhaps she needed to do more research into other cultures and their reverence for nature and approach leaders of these cultures to join in her mission. Well, that would be for another day. Right now, she had to focus on the success of her meeting with Runningwater. As the plane taxied into the gate, Leslie suddenly grew weary. She had not slept much since her encounter with the Matriarch, not wanting to waste a minute of the days that were given to her, and now she wished she was able to sleep on airplanes, but that luxury had always eluded her. Valerie was waiting for her in the baggage claim area. Although she knew Leslie would pack light and not have luggage to retrieve, it was the easiest place to meet. They embraced and Leslie seemed to cling a little tighter than normal. Valerie knew there was something going on in her mother's life, but she also knew Leslie well enough to know that she would clue her in at just the right moment. The two of them had a mutual trust that was rare among mothers and daughters. Valerie had chosen to come to the airport alone rather than bring her family along, just in case there was some exciting news that Leslie wanted to share with her alone. But she could tell by the tiredness around Leslie's eyes, that there would not be any long conversation tonight. She suspected that Leslie would go to bed shortly after dinner, as soon as she had seen all the children and filled the family in briefly about her meeting at Foxwoods.

And, true to form, Valerie had nailed her mother's mood precisely. Leslie, of course, was delighted to see the children, especially little Michael, now seven months old, whom she hadn't seen since she was back in Connecticut when Valerie and Gary came home from the midwife center with newborn Michael, their first son. The three girls, now seven, five and four, of course were always a handful, even for Valerie, who was so well organized that she could handle almost anything life threw her way. She got that from Michael, Leslie was certain. The girls fought for "Nanny's" lap and were eager to see what little trinket she had brought for each of them. Beth, the oldest, was thrilled with the turquoise earrings Nanny had brought her. She had just had her ears pierced for her birthday and, like Leslie, she had already developed a love of cowboys and Indians, so she was happy to get a gift from Nevada that reminded her of the West. Five-year-old Petra was precocious and was able to read well above the level of most five-year-olds, so the little book about desert animals was perfect for her; she could learn how to care for these injured animals when she set up her veterinary clinic in Nevada, close to her Nanny. And precious little Bunny, as her sisters called her, Valerie's Down Syndrome four-year-old, was always so happy to see her grandmother that gifts didn't really matter, but Leslie had brought her a pair of little socks from the Grand Canyon, and a little bag of Ethel M chocolates to share with her sisters. Bunny, whose real name was Barbara, after Gary's grandmother, always loved sharing her gifts with her sisters so Leslie was careful to chose something for her and something she could share. And for Michael, Valerie giggled when she saw Leslie's little cowboy outfit, complete with chaps in a size one-year. Gary would be amused by Leslie's little tricks designed to make his children look like Nevadans. He was sure Leslie would try every trick in the book to get those grandchildren closer to moving west, but Gary hated Nevada and was very happy in their home in West Hartford. He still thought Leslie was a bit crazy to live so far away from her family, but he respected her enough to go along with her little ploys at making cowboys out of his children.

Gary was in the kitchen putting the last minute touches on dinner when they arrived at the house from the airport. His barbequed chicken was a treat Leslie always looked forward to on her visits. He cooked on the gas grill on their patio year round, even when it was too cold to dine outdoors, and tonight, he had a huge pile of chicken breasts marinated in his special secret sauce. They would never eat all that at one sitting, but the leftovers would be great on a tossed salad for Wednesday's lunch. Valerie had made her famous sweet potato salad that she knew Leslie loved and there were fresh melons for dessert. A scrumptious meal indeed!

After all the dinner dishes were cleaned up and Gary had put the girls to bed, they enjoyed their tea in the living room and and Leslie treated herself to a piece of dark organic chocolate that Valerie had bought for the occasion. Leslie told them about her plans for tomorrow, just enough to explain why she was here. They knew she had always cared deeply about the earth and was concerned about what civilization was doing to the environment so they were not surprised to hear about her plans. Alex had been close when he said her trip probably involved asking the Mashantucket Pequots for a donation to one of her causes. Alex had wanted to stop by this evening, but he had to work late on a big client project, so he would be able to take the day off on Wednesday to hear all about Leslie's visit to Foxwoods. Although Leslie didn't go into details about the proposal she would present to Runningwater tomorrow, the plan she talked about made a lot of sense. Gary knew that Leslie had thought this thing out, done all her research and used her connection with Fred Simms to get this appointment.

Before Leslie ran out of steam, Gary made sure to ask, "What time is Fred picking you tomorrow?"

He couldn't resist asking about Fred, because he knew Valerie was concerned but didn't want to bring the subject up tonight. He thought he was being very tactful, asking on the pretext of needing to know if she would join them for breakfast. Gary had decided he would go into work a bit later that morning and make some of his special baked oatmeal with fresh raspberries for breakfast if Leslie was going to be there.

Leslie thought that would be a fine idea,

"Great, Fred isn't picking me up until 10:30. We'll have a quick rest stop on the way down, have lunch at Foxwoods with Runningwater, then I'll meet with Runningwater while Fred confers with the Director of Operations about some casino business. We plan to stop in Norwich for dinner on the way home."

Gary was sure, by the tone of Leslie's voice, that the Fred thing was just a matter of convenience for Leslie to accomplish a higher purpose and assured Valerie later in bed that she didn't have to worry about her mother starting a relationship with Fred.

"In fact," Gary told Valerie, "Fred is too conservative to think about leaving a position with so much job security and a great pension plan, and your mother is certainly not planning to leave Nevada."

"Of course," Valerie reminded him, "she *is* living in the gaming capital of the world and what's to stop Fred from heading to Carson City where he could surely get a job with the Nevada Gaming Commission?"

But Gary was usually pretty accurate in reading her mother and his assurances helped Valerie rest easier.

In the guest room, Leslie pulled out her flannel pajamas and settled under the soft down comforter with her just started copy of *The Female Ancestors of Christ*, but she only got through about four pages when sleep welcomed her into its open arms. She hadn't slept this well in months, and was surprised when the morning sun woke her with the book still lying opened on the bed. She felt wonderfully rested, as though she had slept for weeks. The guest room, which had been Valerie's bedroom when the house still belonged to Leslie and Michael, was sunny and bright and reminded her of Valerie. It hadn't changed much. Leslie showered and dressed quickly, not wanting to miss Gary's baked oatmeal and fresh berries. Two slices of turkey bacon, a cup of herbal green tea and good conversation completed the meal. Gary told Leslie about what was happening at his work and got her caught up on the gossip about her friends at St. Thomas's while Valerie got the kids dressed. After they finished breakfast and Gary had pulled out of the driveway, she and Valerie got the older girls ready for school they loaded Michael into his stroller, with Bunny in the 'rumble seat' and set out for a walk around the neighborhood. They walked as far as St. Joseph's College, where Leslie had worked while her kids were in school and from where Valerie had received her engineering degree. Leslie was glad she had kept that pair of walking shoes at the house for just such an occasion. The morning air felt good and invigorated Leslie to face the day ahead.

She was ready fifteen minutes before Fred rang the bell. As he stepped into the hallway and glimpsed the dining room, Fred remembered the many happy times he and Sally had spent here with Leslie and Michael and had bit of regret that those days were gone. But he looked forward to this day with Leslie, and in fact, was almost giddy as he pulled up to the house. As Leslie came running down the stairs, his heart skipped a beat. She looked fantastic! He had always been amazed at how Leslie could look so good, with seemingly little effort. Sally was always in the bathroom fussing with her hair and makeup, and spent what seemed like hours in the walk-in closet deciding what to wear. Leslie, on the other hand, according to Michael, could jump out of bed, into the shower and be ready to go in about thirty minutes, at least ten of which were spent towel drying her thick, auburn hair.

Now, it seemed to Fred, Leslie looked even younger and prettier than he remembered her. She was dressed casually, but professionally.

Fred, knowing Runningwater as he did, was sure the Pequot casino operator would be enthralled with Leslie. He had made the right decision setting up this appointment and he felt good about the outcome. Leslie grabbed a thermos of freshly brewed, organic, caffeine-free green tea, along with two thermal cups from the Sharper Image she had left at Valerie's house and she put them in her tote bag with the folder for Joseph Runningwater.

On the drive to Mashantucket, Fred filled Leslie in on all their former friends from St. Thomas Church. Although she had heard some of the news from Gary, she was interested in Fred's conversation.

"Father Mulligan is still here, although his health is failing, and the Bishop just sent another assistant to help Mulligan out. Everyone loves Father Morelli, especially the young people who were ready to get more involved in the church but knew that Father Mulligan did not have the energy to start youth programs." Fred told her.

The couples group they had once all been active in had pretty much fallen apart. With Michael's death and Fred and Sally's divorce, the group had started to disintegrate, and then the Callahan's moved to Maine and Bob Marlowe had a stroke. Bev and Bill Ratchett had also been divorced and Bill had moved to upstate New York with his new wife. Leslie felt sad at the thought of how time had dealt these good people such deadly blows.

"Is there any permanence in life anymore?" she asked rather wistfully.

The only couple that seemed not to have had drastic changes in their lives was the Bradys.

"I still golf with Pam and Paul Brady and Father Morelli often makes up the foursome. Of course, they're always wanting to fix me up with a blind date and I have seen Pam's cousin, Shelly, several times."

Leslie remembered Shelly, a pleasant woman, a little overweight but not obese, and she had great eyes and a sparking personality. Leslie always liked Shelly and thought she would be good for Fred. She drew out of Fred that he had given some thought to entering a serious relationship with Shelly, but he admitted he was not in a hurry to get involved again. Fred had taken Sally's infidelity harder than Leslie thought he would. She had not been all that surprised when they announced their separation. Sally had always seemed too self-centered to Leslie and she had often seen her looking at men just a little too long and much too longingly.

Once they got caught up on all their mutual friends, Fred talked about his children.

"Fred Jr. took the divorce hard, and barely speaks to his mother. He's now a successful attorney and I helped him land a job with one of the tribal casinos as their legal counsel. He's moved into his own condo in New Haven and is dating a young attorney who had just made partner in her firm. Roberta will graduate with honors from Yale next year with her degree in international finance."

All was well with the Simms' children.

Leslie told him about her children next. He saw Valerie and her family at 9:00 a.m. mass most weeks and had kept up to date on Leslie's adventures through them.

"Alex has pretty much fallen away from the church and is working way too hard, but otherwise was doing well. Perhaps his new wife will be able to convince him to spend more time with her and less at work," Leslie hoped.

Leslie liked Margaret and felt she would be a good influence on Alex. And Andre would be ordained in a year if all went well. Fred agreed with Leslie that Andre was destined for greatness and would someday be a great leader in the Church.

Leslie couldn't resist the opportunity to boast about her youngest.

"He's at the top of his class in the seminary, just as he had always been in school, and is well liked by his professors and the other seminarians. He'll be coming to spend a few weeks with me as soon as class ends and will then spend his summer working on a reservation in Arizona."

Leslie didn't want to get into the Matriarch experience with Fred at all, so she simply told him that on one of her trips to write an article for a travel magazine, she became inspired to become more deeply involved in her work on conservation. Fred remembered that she had always had a concern about the environment but was amazed to hear the passion in her voice now when she spoke of her ideas and briefly outlined her proposal to Joseph Runningwater. It certainly made a lot of sense to Fred, but he was amazed at how well thought out Leslie's plan was. She obviously had spent a lot of time thinking about this and doing her homework.

"I hope, for your sake, and the sake of the world, that Runningwater will be amenable to your proposal," he said quite sincerely.

By the time they had caught up on all of their family and friends, and discussed the meeting with Runningwater, they had arrived at

Foxwoods. They had planned to meet for lunch in the upscale Chinese restaurant in the casino. Fred thought it was rather ironic that they would be meeting with the Native Americans in a Chinese restaurant, but it was Runningwater's choice. Fred would be sure to find a place with the healthy food he knew Leslie would be more comfortable with on the way home. After lunch, Fred would meet with Jimmy Tall about a problem they were having in filling out the reports for the Keno operation, while Leslie went with Runningwater for a tour of the casino and then on to the meeting to present her ideas.

On the drive to Foxwoods, Leslie couldn't help recalling the trip she and Michael had taken there that September afternoon; it seemed so long ago now! She recalled her amazement when she saw the casino for the first time, out there in the middle of nowhere, surrounded by woods; one would never expect to see such a massive structure in this place. The drive that day had been a relaxing one—the sun was shining brightly and there was a cool fall breeze in the air, hinting of the winter that always seemed to come early in Connecticut. But that day, winter was far from their thoughts as they drove. They had even stopped along the roadside at a picnic table and shared some good Vermont cheddar cheese, flax seed crackers and a bottle of Merlot, topped off with huge, crisp, gala apples. She and Michael had so loved those kinds of days, when there were no family demands, no business calls, just good music on the CD player in the car, good food and wine, and good conversation. She even remembered what they had worn that day—Michael in khakis and a deep red, soft flannel shirt topped with a camel colored crew neck sweater, and she in faded jeans and her favorite cream-colored, Irish cable knit sweater.

The drive today was similar in some ways—the sun was again brightly shining, although spring was in the air now. Fred shared her taste in music and so the CD player filled the car with music much like the songs that she and Michael were listening to that day. But Fred was not Michael, and as pleasant as the drive was, she kept thinking back to happier days.

Once they arrived at Foxwoods, Leslie was again awe-struck by the size of the place, and the fact that it looked so out of place nestled here in the hillsides of Connecticut. She remembered that once she had flown over Foxwoods while traveling to Portland, Maine, from New York, and had thought that it looked even more out of place when you saw it from the air like a fairyland castle not far from the hustle and bustle of Manhattan.

The valet parking attendant opened Leslie's door, took the keys from Fred, and drove away in Fred's shiny new silver Audi. Once inside the door, the magic of the bells and sounds of electronic 'coins' jingling, even though they were now fully automated and no one ever handled real coins anymore, fascinated Leslie. Although she didn't particularly enjoy gambling, the psychology of the gaming industry fascinated her. They did everything they could to enhance the experience and the hope of winning, luring their customers in with flashing lights, computerized games, smiling cocktail waitresses and that sound of winning! She thought how far the Pequots had come from a tribe that was almost nonexistent until they opened this casino. The tribe was now thriving, the museum a tribute to their heritage and their leaders well respected as captains of the Native American gaming industry.

They quickly found their way to the restaurant on the promenade of shops and restaurants that surrounded the casino floor. Runningwater was not there yet but had reserved a quiet corner table for them, and the waiter quickly seated Fred and Leslie. Jimmy Tall was the next to arrive, a short stumpy man, belying his name, with a pock-marked face but beautiful brown eyes and a warm, sincere smile that drew attention away from his skin. Jimmy was good at what he did. He had a mind like a steel trap and nothing escaped from that trap, it seemed. He had a photographic memory and Fred was amazed that he was having problems with the Keno reports. He suspected there was a problem on the Gaming Commission's end; if Jimmy couldn't figure it out, there must be something wrong. Fred often wished Jimmy would come to work for him and had actually tried to lure him away from the Foxwoods' empire, but Jimmy was loyal to Runningwater and to his people. He would never leave Foxwoods, of that Fred was certain, but it didn't hurt to try. Fred introduced Jimmy to Leslie and the two of them seemed to hit it off. Leslie had a deep respect for this man, even though she had never met him, but she had listened to everything Fred had said about him in the car, and she knew that if Fred thought highly of him, he must be good at what he did. Leslie could always make a quick judgment about a person by how they treated those who served them—taxi drivers, waitresses, etc. In fact, she was often criticized for making rash judgments about people before she got to know them, but she had never been proven wrong, so she had never wavered from this habit. And she knew by the way Jimmy talked to the waiter who showed him to their table, that this was a man of good character. He spoke kindly and respectfully to the waiter, asked about his family and thanked the maitre dei, Him Chow, for seating him. She, Fred and Jimmy talked for about ten minutes, small talk mostly about the weather and the casino business in general, before Runningwater strode into the room. It was obvious this was Runningwater, by the way heads turned and waiters stood a little bit taller. Runningwater was as tall as Jimmy Tall was short. He must have been at least 6'4", thought Leslie. And a more handsome man she couldn't recall seeing in a long time. He had jet-black hair and green eyes, and was elegantly dressed in a casual, but obviously very expensive suit, which fit him too well not to have been custom made. His soft white shirt, open at the collar, made his flawless skin look even darker and his teeth may have been the whitest teeth Leslie had ever seen. She could almost see them sparkle, like the television commercials for those whitening procedures, but Leslie was pretty sure Runningwater had not done anything to artificially whiten his teeth.

As opposite as Jimmy Tall and Joseph Runningwater were in looks, Leslie could tell immediately that Runningwater liked and respected Tall. His handshake was warm and genuine and his greeting sincere. He greeted Tall first, and then turned to Fred and gave him the same warm smile and firm handshake. Turning his attention next to Leslie, he extended his hand and when she offered hers in return, he grasped it in both hands and held it for what seemed like ten minutes, although Leslie was certain it couldn't have been more than thirty seconds. Once seated, his height settled comfortably into the leather chair, he was no less impressive. He was the center of attention everywhere he went, of this Leslie was convinced. In fact, Leslie was almost dumbstruck and wondered how she would get through her well-planned presentation to Runningwater. She sensed that Runningwater was well aware of his effect on people and had planned this lunch to allow enough time for Leslie to get comfortable with him. Why on earth hadn't Fred warned her about this? Why had he described Runningwater only by saying he was a smart man, one who revered his family and his people and who was well respected in the industry. It took Leslie a good five minutes to feel at ease enough to even speak. And that was a very rare emotion for her. She was accustomed to speaking before crowds and had never had a problem talking to people one-on-one. She had never hesitated to approach anyone, anywhere, no matter what his or her position. She had spoken at town meetings, facilitated workshops, was a lector in church, led study groups, taught classes and had never been at a loss for words anywhere. But there was something about Joseph Runningwater that left her feeling somehow inadequate. She felt a fleeting resentment towards Fred for arranging this meeting without fully preparing her. Fred looked a bit surprised by Leslie's obvious feeling of awkwardness. But Runningwater was the consummate gentleman. Detecting Leslie's nervousness, he immediately put her at ease by asking about her horse, Mancha. She had no idea how he even knew she owned horses, let alone her special friend and kindred spirit, Mancha.

Once the subject of horses was raised, Leslie immediately relaxed and she and Joseph spent the next twenty minutes or so talking about their favorite horses while Fred and Jimmy talked about the casino and the museum. Lunch arrived and Leslie suddenly felt famished. Joseph seemed delighted that she enjoyed her meal so thoroughly; he was proud of his restaurants, but always worried that the food wasn't quite good enough for his guests with discriminating taste. He scowled just slightly when Leslie asked for hot water to brew her own special tea, knowing the typical Chinese tea was never caffeine free. She, of course, did not tell Joseph that she was using a detoxifying tea to overcome the toxins that were usually found in restaurant food, except when she could find an organic restaurant.

He brightened considerably when she assured him, "This Bird Nest soup is the best I've ever tasted."

She went on to explain, "I'm sorry about the tea, but I'm allergic to caffeine and I do love my tea, so I always carry my own since most restaurant's don't provide it."

It was easier to explain away her preferences by saying she had food allergies; people always had more sympathy for people with allergies than they did for picky eaters.

Runningwater made a mental note to provide caffeine-free, green tea in his restaurants, along with raw sugar for those health conscious people that might visit his facility. Observing Leslie's eating habits and noting her trim figure, he asked the waiter to find some perfect fresh fruit for dessert for Leslie and she was delighted by a perfectly presented plate of fresh strawberries, raspberries and kiwi fruit drizzled with just a hint of dark, sweet chocolate, which she indulged in with relish while the men enjoyed the specialty of the house, crème brulee, an interesting selection she didn't expect to be offered in a Chinese restaurant.

Once dessert was consumed and more tea was served, the waiter having discreetly brought Leslie a pot which he had brewed from her own tea bag, Jimmy was ready to get down to business and suggested that he and Fred adjourn to his office. Runningwater was pleased to see them head off to conduct their business, as he was eager to take Leslie on the grand tour. It wasn't often he had such a delightful woman to whom he could show off his empire, and one who was a skilled horsewoman at that. He had been riding since before he could walk, it seemed, and horses were his big passion.

He had done his homework and checked up on Leslie as soon as Fred had called him. Fred had explained that Leslie had lived in Hartford for many years, that she was now a widow and had moved to Nevada and that she had four horses, but he wanted to know more. He put our feelers with his friends in the gaming community in Nevada and with the Reno Sparks Indian Colony and he found out more about Leslie than she would ever imagine. He still wasn't sure exactly what she had in mind, but he had a general idea, and the thought had intrigued him. Now that he had met Leslie, he was even more intrigued.

Runningwater had spent most of his adulthood working in the gaming industry and become the poster boy for what a young Indian boy, in trouble with drugs and alcohol at an early age, could do with his life when he made up his mind. He credited his turnaround to a young priest who was his sociology professor at Seton Hall, where he had received a scholarship. Despite his addictions, he was a brilliant student and good at sports, so it was fairly easy for him to get into a good school. Father Melendez had a rough start in life himself and took Runningwater under his wing soon after his arrival at Seton Hall. For a while, Runningwater even considered the priesthood himself, but his good looks and charm made it hard for him to think about celibacy. He'd been fighting off girls since first grade, and college girls were no different than the high school girls who called him incessantly. He knew he could not give up that life for the Church, so he continued on with his business and finance courses and graduated summa cum laude after just three and half years, and went straight on to get his masters in business administration from Yale immediately after graduation. Of course, as it turned out, his career now took up so much of his time, that he had no time for women anyway and hadn't dated anyone seriously since college. His gratitude to Father Melendez had been a big part of his life and he continued to make substantial donations to the Church as his success grew. Knowing Leslie had a son in the seminary made her even more interesting to Runningwater. He would have to ask about Andre once they had finished their tour.

The tour was an eye opener for Leslie. She thought she had seen enough casinos to last her a lifetime, living in Nevada, especially when most of her friends from back east visited and wanted to see all the action in town. But this place was amazing to Leslie. As they walked through the casino floor, Runningwater handed her a fifty-dollar bill and insisted she try her luck at the Mega Millions machine. She had never even considered playing a $1 slot machine, but she humored him. He wanted to see which machine she would choose. *Wheel of Fortune* was the most popular among the dollar machines, but he knew Leslie would choose something more unique. She looked around the floor, somehow sensing that this was a test, and then she spotted a machine featuring Native American symbols and it actually had horses on it, Leopard Appaloosas of all things, so of course that was her choice. She slipped the bill into the slot on the machine, pulled the handle a few times, and won $100, then $40 and she wanted to quit, but she could see he was enjoying watching her, and besides, she had gotten close to the big jackpot several times, the Buffalo symbol coming up on the top and bottom lines but not in the center where it counted. Just like the compulsive gamblers who filled the casino here as they did in Reno and Vegas, she played off her winnings until she had spent it all.

Runningwater laughed and said, "That's how we get rich here."

After her gambling adventure, he took her behind the scenes to the money room, the vault, the security room and the accounting department. This was quite an operation. And it was obvious how much his employees loved and respected Runningwater. Women and men alike seemed captivated by him; his charisma was overwhelming. Finally, it was time to head to the executive offices and here Leslie was even more awe-struck. The reception area was quiet and plush, the exact opposite of the casino floor where everything jingled and lights blared. This room was dimly lit with recessed lighting and a huge bronze statue of an eagle filled one corner of the reception area. Etched glass doors and rich, burled wood, hunter green soft carpets that must have been several inches thick made Leslie suddenly so drowsy she felt she could just curl up on that carpet and take a nap, it was so peaceful here. There was soft Native American music coming from speakers that she could not see and the place smelled like a pine forest with a hint of fresh rainwater. A waterfall covered one whole wall, softly trickling over polished stones. A small blonde woman, impeccably dressed, sat behind the reception desk. Her small, wire-framed glasses were perched on the end of her nose. She was probably fifty if she was a day, but she looked like she wasn't yet thirty. Her black wool suit and while silk blouse made Leslie suddenly feel underdressed. However, Andrea, as Runningwater addressed her, got up and greeted Leslie warmly, asking if she could bring her water, coffee, a cocktail, or if she would like to use the powder room. Leslie took Andrea up on the offer of the restroom. She felt she might need to splash some cold water on her face to bring her back to reality, and she asked for some bottled water.

When she came back from the ladies' room, which was indeed a luxurious facility, although she suspected that other than Andrea, there were not too many women who used this spacious facility, Andrea escorted her into Joseph's office. His office was larger than Leslie's living room, dining room and kitchen combined. It was tastefully decorated of course, but almost sparse, with expensive leather sofas lining two walls and a small conference table with six leather chairs. On the center of the table were three plain glass vases of different heights with several inches of amber glass beads and each with an orange tiger lily at a various stage of opening. Runningwater's desk was massive but tasteful, dark cherry wood and completely bare except for a small flat screen computer and a leather appointment book with a gold Mont Blanc pen clipped to it. Behind the desk, on a matching credenza, were his Blackberry in its cradle and a metal sculpture depicting the Pequots battling the Metuoc, the tribe they defeated enabling them to be the sole traders with the Dutch invaders. It was, Leslie thought, a tribute to the business acumen of the Pequots, which had carried over to the present day and Runningwater was the prime example of the Pequot skill in sales and marketing. In a corner was another waterfall—six pieces of beautiful terra cotta pottery with water lazily drifting from the largest to the smallest piece. Behind the conference table was a set of French doors opening out onto a balcony with a magnificent view of the museum and the woods surrounding it.

On the conference table, where Joseph was already seated, were two bottled waters, Voss sparkling artesian water from Norway, in tall, slender glass containers with silver lids, shaped like the vases on the table, and two crystal glasses centered on simple but expensive, sterling silver coasters. No Dinsani or Fuji water in plastic bottles here! Joseph stood up as Leslie entered the room and showed her to the seat next to his at the conference table. But she couldn't take her seat just yet; she was spellbound by what hung on the walls of his office. His choice in artwork was the biggest surprise of the day. On one wall was an Edgar Degas—*The Laundress*. Leslie wondered how he had obtained it. She was sure she had seen it in a museum somewhere and yet, she knew this was the original because Joseph would not have a copy in his office. On another wall, a massive scene depicting the Pequot village with a chief who looked amazingly like Runningwater himself—a revered ancestor or an egotistic rendition of himself? But the piece Leslie's eyes had been drawn to immediately— a picture of a bristlecone pine. Her heart was beating so hard she thought she might faint when she saw this unique photograph and Runningwater picked up immediately on her fascination with this piece of art.

"Methuselah," he said, "the oldest living thing on Earth."

"I know," Leslie replied in a whisper; she could hardly breathe.

How did he know? But of course, he didn't know. It was a coincidence; it had to be.

"You've seen it?" he asked.

"No, I missed it, but I have been to the forest and seen the others."

She couldn't bring herself to even mention the Matriarch. She needed some time to catch her breath and she wished she could have crawled under the soft fleece throw that was thrown over the back of one of the leather sofas and taken a nap. Although Runningwater himself would have preferred snuggling on the leather sofa and looking out the window at the rolling Connecticut Hills of Stonington, he knew it was time to get down to business with Leslie. She knew it too, and recovered enough to pull the proposal from her leather tote bag. She sipped some of the water as she shook the cobwebs from her mind and cleared her throat.

Her nervousness had ceased as the tour progressed, and she felt she really had bonded with Runningwater. Despite his wealth and good looks, he was as down to earth as she was. Their shared love for horses and for the earth, and now the bristlecone pines, had cemented their friendship even though they had only known each other a few hours. It was as though they had somehow known each other in another life. Leslie thought about her Native American roots, and although she could not really explain her experience with the Matriarch to him, she thought that he was somehow aware of her ancestry and felt this kinship because of it. They had talked during the tour about their mutual concern for the environment and this was her opening, to build further on the rapport the two of them shared by verbalizing this shared concern. She addressed the issue of how together they could stop the massive destruction of the earth that they both feared.

She laid out her plan, showing him the graphs and charts she had printed in soft earth tones in her proposal. Leslie had done her homework, down to showing the revenues for every Native American casino in the country, the number of guests served, the number of jackpots paid out, the fees generated by the entertainment and ancillary interests of the gaming industry; it was all there in graphs and charts. She could see he was impressed with her work. When she had finished, he didn't have many questions. It was almost as if he had been expecting everything she presented. She sensed a mysterious quality in Runningwater that made her feel he could read her mind; perhaps he had had a premonition or vision about this meeting before it happened. For a minute she could picture him as a shaman, leading his people towards water, healing the sick, standing on a great mountain and prophesying. The words about returning the Church to the mystics and prophets rang through her mind. Was Runningwater to fulfill all of the edicts she had been handed on that mountaintop? But for now, her concern was protecting creation. And she could tell she had made the right choice coming to Foxwoods. She felt sure Runningwater would approve her plan and would help carry it out. Her plan was simple, although monumental. She has asked Runningwater to serve as chairperson of a campaign that would channel millions, maybe billions of gaming revenues into saving the environment. It made sense that the Native American casino owners would lead this campaign. Who more than the Native Americans had this love for the earth and all it held? With Runningwater's support, she was certain the other Native American casinos would get behind this project. The plan called for every Native American casino to set aside a percentage of all their revenues to be put into an endowment that would fund the National Park Service, The Nature Conservancy, researchers and other environmental groups chosen by the Creation Foundation, which would be established by Foxwoods and other leaders of the Native American gaming community. Not only would this be a fundraising campaign, but a public awareness campaign as well. Each casino would sign a pledge to use only earth-friendly products in all their hotels and casinos. They would ask guests to conserve as well, and ask them to contribute a portion of all their winnings to the Creation Foundation. In fact, a brochure about the Creation Foundation would be handed to every winner of a jackpot over $1,200 when they were handed their IRS tax form, a great incentive to make a gift. All entertainers and sports stars that performed or played in any of the casinos would agree to donate a portion of their fees as well. Just one major boxing match could bring in a million dollars to the cause. Leslie was sure that once this campaign was announced, the gaming interests in Nevada and other states would get on the bandwagon as well. They were already losing too much money to the Native American casinos and they would not want to be outdone by these guys again.

Runningwater loved the plan; he agreed to head up the project and vowed to get his attorneys working on establishing the Creation Foundation right away. He would plan a council of all his fellow Native American casino owners and have Leslie come give her presentation to them, complete with PowerPoint slides and graphs on poster boards. He would serve a Native American meal at the museum and all the amenities would be earth-friendly. The plan was so simple and yet they were both certain it would work. It would create international interest in conservation activities.

As the meeting concluded, both Leslie and Joseph were giddy with the possibilities. Using the casino profits to help save the earth was something that he had wanted to do for a long time but was not sure how to go about it, and now here was this beautiful, sincere, enthusiastic woman with the answer! And the knowledge that he would be working closely with Leslie throughout the next year to put the plan in motion was not a small matter to him. He was looking forward to getting to know her better. And Leslie was amazed at how easy it had been; how Runningwater had caught her enthusiasm and heightened it with his own. As Leslie rose, she began to extend her hand for Joseph to shake it. He, uncharacteristically, embraced her warmly and kissed her on both cheeks. He wasn't sure what had gotten into him. Displays of affection were not easy for him, but there was something about this woman that made it seem very natural to embrace her. He hesitated a few seconds and then opened his wallet. Leslie hoped he wasn't going to hand her another $50 bill and tell her to try her luck one more time. But he pulled a well-worn piece of paper from the leather billfold, one that she could tell he had opened and read time after time.

"I would like you to have this," he whispered.

Leslie could tell it was a difficult thing for him to give up, far more difficult than if he had handed her several of the hundred dollar bills she was certain lined that wallet. She didn't know if she should open it and read it right away, defer opening it until she got outside the door or wait until she was in the car with Fred. But in her typical impulsive manner, she carefully unfolded it standing there in front of him. On the paper was a typed poem, which she read quietly to herself.

> *Listen to the air.*
> *You can hear it, feel it,*
> *smell it, taste it.*
> *Woniya Wakan, the holy air,*
> *which renews all by its breath,*
> *Woniya Wakan, spirit, life, breath, river,*
> *it means all that.*
> *We sit together, don't touch,*
> *but something is there,*
> *we feel it between us,*
> *as a presence.*
> *A good way to start thinking about nature,*
> *talk about it.*
> *Rather, talk to it,*
> *talk to the river, to the lakes,*
> *to the winds,*
> *as to our relationship.*
> *John Lame Deer, Lakota*

Leslie felt a tear running down her cheek. She didn't want to deprive him of the pleasure he obviously received by giving her the poem, and yet she hesitated to accept it from him, knowing it meant so much to him. But it was the perfect way to sum up their meeting, so she carefully folded it back up and opened her wallet, inserting it in a special place from which she knew she would never remove it.

Without speaking, they both glanced at the photograph of Methuselah and spoke almost in unison.

"Someday, I will tell you more about that."

Leslie had recovered from the shock of the poem and the comment about Methuselah and was just about walking on air when she met Fred in the lobby, twenty minutes late, but Fred didn't seem to mind. He had been enjoying a Starbucks latte and the company of a cocktail waitress dressed as an Indian princess. He acted a bit embarrassed when he spotted Leslie bouncing towards him. He could see her face was flushed and her eyes were beaming, so he knew the meeting went well, and he couldn't wait to hear the details over dinner. Leslie gave him the thumbs up sign while she was still a good twenty feet from him and as she got closer, he opened his arms, knowing she was going to hug him. She felt warm and soft and smelled of Runningwater's musky cologne. Fred felt a momentary pang of jealousy, knowing he certainly couldn't compete with this handsome, wealthy and suave Native American if he needed to, but he couldn't worry about that possibility now, and wasn't even sure he wanted to think that far. He was still hurting from Sally's infidelity and didn't think he was ready to jump into a relationship, even with Leslie, whom he had known for so long.

Once they retrieved Fred's Audi from the valet parking service, they headed back onto Route 2 towards Norwich, where they had planned to stop for an early dinner. Leslie was unusually quiet on the drive until they had settled into a corner table in the small, cozy restaurant Fred often stopped at on his drive home from Foxwoods. Leslie could not, would not share the poem or many of the details of her meeting with Fred or anyone else, but she was eager to tell him about Joseph' reaction to her proposal.

"He loved it and is eager to help get things rolling," she had told him as they were driving.

Now, she shared the details of the plan with Fred. Runningwater had some ideas of his own that Leslie hadn't even considered. One that she found quite exciting was that he planned to talk to his suppliers from Nevada about designing a special *Friends of Creation* slot machine which would have reels with oceans, rivers, lakes, trees and endangered species and would have a higher than normal payout rate in order to attract customers to play it. They would try to get these machines placed in every casino in the country, Native American and others, and each casino would donate the entire proceeds of these machines to the Foundation. Winners of jackpots on these machines would be given a special treatment by the casinos, a free room anytime they wanted it, free dinners during every stay, as a reward for agreeing to donate ten percent of their jackpot winnings to the Foundation. There would be a guaranteed jackpot winner every week. Like other big money machines, they would all be hooked up to a central computer so proceeds could be tracked and a check sent to the Foundation every week. Fred was intrigued by the details of Leslie's proposal, down to special merchandise in all the casino gift shops, the use of all earth-friendly products in the hotel rooms and the proceeds of sporting and entertainment events also being tapped into. He thought this plan could revolutionize the entertainment industry and knowing how Americans were influenced by the 'cause celebre' phenomenon, he could see many of these entertainers encouraging support of environmental projects all over the world.

The next couple of months were busy ones for Leslie and Runningwater, and for Fred and Jimmy Tall as well, who had been enlisted to help. In fact, Leslie had recommended that Fred be hired to serve as Executive Director of the Foundation, a concept that Runningwater fully endorsed. He had always been impressed with Simms and had tried, on numerous occasions, to lure him away from the state government to come to work for him. Runningwater's trip to Reno to meet with the slot machine manufacturers, of course involved a visit with Leslie. They went horseback riding, hiked the trails and visited Pyramid Lake. They had talked about even taking a trip to the Ancient Bristlecone Pine Forest but Leslie knew she couldn't go there with Runningwater or anyone else, at least not yet. She still had not actually seen Methuselah and the offer was tempting, but Runningwater was short on time and in the back of his head, he thought, "well, another reason to come back here and see Leslie again." Fred moved the Foundation along even quicker than any of them had expected. It paid to have connections in the hierarchy of the governmental maze and the 501 (c) (3) PF status was received in record time. He found an office suite in New Haven and hired an assistant. Valerie agreed to help him select furniture and a computer system. Alex even got involved in helping him find accountants and attorneys who specialized in foundation work.

Runningwater and Leslie spent a great deal of their time emailing each other to plan their meeting with all the leaders of the tribal casinos and Valerie helped her put her presentation into PowerPoint format. A big launching event was planned for Labor Day weekend. The event planners at Foxwoods were all on overtime to assure every detail was handled to perfection. Although they didn't know all the details of this event, they knew it was the most important thing Runningwater had ever asked them to plan, and if it was important to him, it was equally vital to them.

Chapter 14

Vatican City

George had finally decided to call Leslie. She was sorry she hadn't emailed, but she was engrossed in a major project. She couldn't tell George about the whole experience just yet, but she knew that would come soon. She still had to sort things out. Her whole experience with Fred and Joseph Runningwater had left her exhausted, not just because of the tension she felt from working on and presenting her proposal, but because with her heightened sensitivity to the thoughts of those around her, she knew that both men were attracted to her. She had always sensed this about Fred, but his thoughts in the car and during their dinner were a bit frightening. First of all, he seemed to think that she was attracted to Runningwater and he was jealous of this man, even if he wasn't ready yet himself to declare his feelings to Leslie. There was some tension during lunch that first day between Simms and Runningwater, so Leslie had been relieved when she and Fred went their separate ways, Fred with Jimmy Tall to talk business, and she with Joseph Runningwater to present her proposal. In the car that evening on their way back to Hartford, she again felt this fear coming from Fred that he was somehow losing her, even before they had time to start a relationship. But during her explanation of Runningwater's enthusiasm for her plan, she felt Fred lighten up. He was truly glad to see this idea of hers so well received and was already thinking about how he might fit into the plan. In fact, the idea of him being the Executive Director of the Foundation had actually come to Leslie through Fred's thoughts, if not his words.

Leslie did tell George about her plan, at least in a cursory way. She skipped over the part about how this idea had come to her, so George mistakenly assumed that she had formed a relationship with someone from one of the Reno casinos, probably a woman she met at church, who was concerned about how they might best use their charitable dollars. Knowing of Leslie's love for nature, it was no surprise to George that she had come up with this plan, but the extent of it amazed him. She was bubbling with enthusiasm for the Foundation and told him about Fred—how he had introduced her to Runningwater and that he was giving up his job with the Connecticut Gaming Commission to become Executive Director of the Creation Foundation. George was intrigued, but not surprised by the name of the Foundation she and Runningwater had already established. He remembered her fascination with Michelangelo's depiction of the Creation. In fact, he recalled how in their youth she had argued with him that there was something wrong with this painting. If Adam was truly the first man, created by God, he shouldn't have a belly button, argued a precocious ten-year-old Leslie, because it indicated Adam came from a human mother or at least had an umbilical cord. George had always been amazed at the things his sister questioned, and to this day was still amazed at some of the thoughts that she revealed to him. He wondered how wise it was for Fred Simms to up and quit his job, with children in college, but apparently Leslie had convinced him this plan would work. George was certain of her powers of persuasion, having been the recipient, and sometimes the victim, of her tenacity and charisma himself on numerous occasions. And apparently Runningwater was funding this Foundation so he must be convinced as well. Leslie promised to email George a copy of her proposal and she hoped he might take time away from his busy schedule to attend the event they had planned in September. In the back of Leslie's mind, of course, was all the Vatican money that might be channeled into this project as well.

As was often the case in their conversations, there was a lot unsaid by Leslie that George always managed to fill in, and usually he was right on target, although this time, he missed some of the key points. He could tell that Leslie was holding something back and, again mistakenly, thought there was either a relationship beginning with Runningwater or with Simms. His bet was on Runningwater; he could sense a special tone in Leslie's voice when she mentioned his name, almost a reverence. He promised her that he would do his best to fly to Connecticut for her big event, and answered her questions about what was happening in his life and in the Vatican. After a brief update on all her children, especially Andre, they hung up since it was already late evening for Leslie when he had called.

Although George had not filled her in totally on what was happening at the Vatican, he did think that the Connecticut trip in September would be a welcome change. Things had been pretty stressful for him the last month or so. His archrival, Ferranti, was becoming more and more of a problem for John XXIV and for Castle. His latest endeavor was to try to gather enough support from the Cardinals to try to reverse the Pope's decision to ordain openly gay men. He had mustered support from many of the Italian Cardinals and some of the other Europeans, but the Americans, as usual, were forming a solid block of opposition against Ferranti. And of course, the Dutch supported what Ferranti considered to be John XXIV's lunacy.

George had been busy trying to accomplish routine work in the midst of all this. Their work on the AIDS project for instance, had been slowed to almost a halt because many of the cardinals still thought of AIDS as a gay man's disease, and saw any support of the AIDS project as support for homosexuality. George had worked with the Vatican researchers to develop a position that clearly separated the two issues by pointing out the statistics that proved the majority of new AIDS cases were women and children. Brother Rocco Brunetti had been more than helpful to George in preparing his case for the cardinals. Brunetti was one of the best researchers in the world. He could find statistics online for just about anything. Not only could he find them, but also he had a knack of translating statistics in a realistic and yet persuasive manner. He was able to put together graphs and charts that even an illiterate person could grasp, and his work on this project proved exemplary. George was certain that once he had made his presentation to the Cardinals, they would support this important project, saving millions of lives. The Pope was committed to pouring millions of dollars into education and prevention, starting with Africa and the United States and eventually worldwide. George had planned to meet privately with the most influential Cardinals to enlist their support before making his formal presentation to the entire Council, which would be held next month. He was finding his days filled with the intrigue that typically was part of all big decisions at the Vatican, and now with this issue of Ferranti constantly undermining his efforts, the process was moving even slower than normal. It seemed as though Ferranti somehow had George's schedule at his fingertips and followed every one of George's visits with one of his own, counteracting much of what George had accomplished. It was several weeks into George's plan before he realized Ferranti was his shadow, following quickly on his footsteps with every Cardinal. He found out quite by accident when his visit with Cardinal Mulholland of Ireland had to be rescheduled from Tuesday to a Thursday, and when he sat down across from Mulholland, an old friend and ally, Mulholland presented him with a folder Ferranti had given him the day before. Ferranti had seemed surprised that Castle had not yet been to see Mulholland, but launched into his tirade anyway, arguing against points that Mulholland had not yet heard from Castle. The whole meeting seemed to upset Ferranti. He obviously had come prepared to follow up on Castle's presentation and have the last word, as would a defense attorney in a trial. Ferranti obviously thought of himself as the chief defender of the faith and was prepared to do anything to defeat the assault on his faith he felt John XXIV and Cardinal Castle were committing.

Mulholland and Castle chuckled over Ferranti's frustration caused by this delayed meeting. Although the presentation that Ferranti had handed Mulholland would surely have landed in George's hands eventually, of this Ferranti was sure, he was highly displeased that it was presented prior to Castle's visit with Mulholland. Ironically, it had been Ferranti himself that had caused the appointment to be rescheduled, which made it even more ironic and more humorous to the two friends. Castle had planned to see Mulholland on Tuesday morning just before lunch, but Monday afternoon, Castle's secretary had text-messaged him that John XXIV needed to talk with him by phone that morning. He had gotten wind of Ferranti's scheme through his friend Brunetti who had pieced together the plot based on the research Ferranti had been doing in the Vatican Library, with assistance from Brunetti's subordinate, Father Morelli. Castle had canceled the meeting with Mulholland so he could spend that hour working on his email to the Pope who was traveling in Zaire and Zimbabwe. Mulholland of course understood when George had called his secretary to reschedule the meeting for Thursday afternoon. In fact they used the opportunity to schedule the meeting late in the day and have dinner together afterwards.

Mulholland had no compulsion about sharing Ferranti's information with Castle. They each disliked the man intensely and were more than a little concerned about his devious approach. The two friends compared notes on what they knew about Ferranti and his latest attack on the Pope. They spent an hour and half reviewing George's meetings so far and the response he had gotten from the Cardinals he had spoken with and then speculating about what happened in the meetings with Ferranti that, as George was now aware, had followed quickly on the heels of his meetings with each Cardinal. They created a list of those Cardinals that they felt now needed a second meeting with George and, although Mulholland was willing to help in any way, George knew this was something he had to do himself. He would now be several weeks behind schedule and would have to schedule meetings in the evening and early morning. There was no choice but to put in longer hours than he had planned, leaving little time for his other work. Mulholland, however, could help him with some of the other tasks on his plate, like meeting with some of the delegations from around the world that came to present themselves and their pleas to the Pope. Before they adjourned for an early dinner they both felt better about the plan they had conceived. It was during dinner that Mulholland revealed a plan even more frightening than the thought of Ferranti winning over a sufficient number of Cardinals to defeat the Pope's AIDS plan.

Mulholland was convinced that Ferranti was actually plotting to overthrow the Pope, something unheard of since the Middle Ages. The signs were all there. Ferranti openly spoke to the press and the public about the heresies he felt John XXIV had committed against the Church. He was trying to gather enough supporters around him so that when the Council met next month, he could make his move. Mulholland had observed him in the library talking with Morelli, Brunetti's assistant, knowing the two librarians had a totally opposite theology. Brunetti was a liberal who was sympathetic to the changes this Pope was bringing about. He was eager to help Castle and the Pope with their fight to assure that the Church took up the social causes endorsed by the Liberation theologians who had been silenced by earlier Popes. Morelli, on the other hand, was extremely conservative and Ferranti was sure that he could convince Morelli to help him assemble the materials needed to fight his battle with these heretics. What Ferranti had not counted on was Morelli's obedience to Church hierarchy and, as a result, his confiding in Brunetti. Ferranti also did not count on Morelli's fear and dislike of him. While he respected the Church hierarchical system too much to argue with Ferranti or to deny him access to the research at which he and Brunetti were so adept, he also was conservative enough to believe wholeheartedly in supporting whoever currently sat in the Chair of Peter and would never do anything to cause trouble for the Holy Father.

Morelli had first met Ferranti while Ferranti was Archbishop of Milan and had come to Rome to do research in the Vatican Library. Ferranti was known to be an expert in Canon Law, and the reason for his visit, Morelli was certain, was to undermine the Vatican II reforms.

While Morelli agreed with Ferranti on this subject, he was also certain that Ferranti had purposely sought him out, knowing he would be sympathetic to Ferranti's requests. However, the minute Ferranti walked into the library, Morelli despised the man. Perhaps it was because his physical appearance reminded Morelli of his own father, whom he despised.

Morelli had grown up in Rome and had wanted to be a priest ever since he could remember. His father hated the Church and all it stood for, and he didn't want his son to have anything to do with it. His father beat his mother so badly she had a limp as a result of one of his drunken tirades. Morelli never knew what caused his father's bitterness towards the Church, but he suspected that a member of the clergy had abused him during his childhood. When his father died at the age of thirty eight from the damage he had done to his liver, along with the battering he had received during several barroom brawls, Morelli did not grieve for his father, but only for his mother who would now be forced to work even harder that before to support their little family. By the time Morelli was ready to leave home and enter the seminary at the age of fourteen, his mother was dying. He had so hoped she could live to see her son become a priest, but the constant beatings, lack of proper diet and breathing the smoke that Morelli's father had filled the house with during every waking moment, proved too much for her.As she slipped into a coma, she pressed the rosary she had made as a little girl into her son's hand and begged him to keep his promise to her to become a priest and to always remain faithful to his vow of celibacy.

But it wasn't just Ferranti's appearance that bothered Morelli; it was his attitude. He was the most condescending man Morelli had ever met, and he had met his share during his days in the seminary. As Ferranti placed his books on the library counter, he dropped one, and stood there waiting for Morelli to come around the counter and pick it up. Morelli thought for minute about just letting it lie there and pretending he hadn't seen it, ignoring the glaring look Ferranti was riveting him with because he had hesitated too long. But this was, after all, an Archbishop, and he was a young priest who knew his place so he quickly opened the small gate that separated him from this distasteful man, picked up the book and placed it on the counter on top of the others.

"Oh, did I drop that?" Ferranti said with a smirk, as though he hadn't noticed.

Morelli would like to have just told Ferranti that he was busy and he would have to come back, but he knew he couldn't do that.

"No problem, Your Eminence," Morelli deferred.

He listened attentively as Ferranti read off his list of requests and went to find the numerous volumes Ferranti had asked him to retrieve.

Now, Morelli was caught in a morass of his loyalty to the Church, his belief that this Pope was too liberal, his fear for the current Holy Father's position, and his distaste for Ferranti. His fear and loyalty won out and he went to Brunetti to discuss his fears that Ferranti was up to something. Brunetti agreed and decided to talk to Mulholland about this impending disaster. He and Mulholland had conferred on several occasions about Ferranti and others that they felt were harming the Church and perhaps plotting against the Pope. After hearing Brunetti's concern, Mulholland determined that he should talk to Castle about this. However, before he had an opportunity to plan his approach to Castle, he had received the call from Castle himself, to set up their meeting for this past Tuesday. Mulholland was disappointed when Castle had to reschedule, because he was eager to share his fears with someone else, and he was sure that Castle would agree that they needed to do something about Ferranti. Then, when Ferranti had called the same afternoon that he and Castle had set their original meeting, Mulholland was really concerned. What on earth did Ferranti want? Did he suspect that Mulholland had talked to Morelli and was he coming there to explain himself?

Tuesday afternoon was the day Mulholland generally spent catching up on correspondence, and although he tried to hide his annoyance at Ferranti for disturbing his routine, he was probably not the most gracious of hosts that afternoon. He offered Ferranti his own special blend of Irish tea and imported scones, as was customary for him to do with afternoon visitors, but he almost wished Ferranti had said no, not wanting to break bread with the man. Ferranti, of course, eagerly accepted his offer and while they were waiting for Mulholland's assistant to bring the refreshments, they made small talk about the renovations that were currently underway in the Vatican. Pope John XXIV had wanted a simpler décor and had moved several pieces of art into the Vatican Museum from their places within the Papal offices. Ferranti was outraged that some of the beautiful works of the old masters were being replaced by African Art and American Art, but that day, with Mulholland, he tried to hide his anger and talk about the improvements that were being made within the museum itself, an updated climate control system, an improved security system, and a new educational wing. John XXIV wanted the artwork not just to be admired, but for people to learn about its origins and meaning. He also planned to bring in more contemporary religious art to the museum. Ferranti was fearful that he would add some of the ridiculous pieces those crazy Americans called art, like a crucifixion portraying Jesus as a woman. But today, he kept his discussion light and focused on neutral issues, which he knew Mulholland and he agreed on, like the need for the improved climate control and security systems. Terrorist threats on the Vatican had led to an overall increase in security, and safeguarding the museum was of prime importance, lest the treasures of the Church be stolen and sold on the black market or worse yet desecrated by these Godless vandals.

Once the tea and scones arrived, Mulholland and Ferranti settled into the two burgundy leather wing backed chairs that sat by the window, normally one of Mulholland's favorite places to sit and view the piazza below. Today, however, with the silver tea service between them on the small round mahogany table, Mulholland felt as far apart from Ferranti as two human beings could possibly be. Even their small talk had been strained and Mulholland was eager for Ferranti to get down to business and tell him why he was here. Ferranti, sensing Mulholland's impatience, opened his small, well-worn, tan leather briefcase and pulled from it a small black folder. He thought that Castle had been here before him to present the Pope's plan for solving the AIDS issue, so he started right into his dialogue about the frivolity of this plan. One could not solve a problem of this level by throwing money at it, and the Church's money could be used for much better purposes. As he leafed through the folder, pointing out to Mulholland each point in his own plan, he came to realize that Mulholland had not yet talked with Castle. This was disastrous! Now Castle would be coming in to see Mulholland with the advantage of seeing Ferranti's plans. He knew that even if Castle had been here first, Mulholland would have called him the minute Ferranti stepped outside the door to tell him what Ferranti was up to. But it was a chance he had to take. He could not gain enough support from the other Cardinals without the influence of Mulholland and, although he doubted he could sway Mulholland to his way of thinking, he knew that Mulholland would give him a fair chance to present his case and that he would also assure him a fair hearing at the Council. Perhaps if Mulholland had met with Castle first, he would have taken all of this with a grain of salt and would have dismissed Ferranti's ramblings as futile. But, hearing his side of the issue first had a sobering effect on Mulholland. This man was dangerous, to the Pope, to the Church and to the world if he had his way.

Mulholland now shared with Castle that he was convinced there was more to this latest posturing of Ferranti against the Pope's AIDS plan than met the eye. The fact that Ferranti seemed to know Castle's comings and goings on a daily basis meant he had been doing some espionage. Mulholland told Castle about his conversations with Brunetti in the Vatican Library and related what Brunetti had learned from Morelli.

"This man is up to no good," insisted Mulholland. "He has been researching Canon Law and the Popes of the Middle Ages, and last month, he asked Morelli to research the removal of Popes. I think the reason he is so quick to share the dissenting viewpoint he will present to the Council about the Pope's AIDS project, is because he wants to throw us off track. He has bigger fish to fry."

Castle couldn't believe his ears. Would Ferranti actually try to persuade the Council to remove the Pope? This was beyond belief. And yet, it made sense. Thinking back to some of the comments Ferranti had openly made about the Pope and about Castle himself, there was no question Ferranti believed in his heart that there were heretics rampant in the Vatican and that John XXIV was the greatest heretic of them all. Castle and Mulholland spent hours talking that evening over their after dinner brandy and several of Mulholland's disgusting cigars. If it weren't for those damn cigars, he would be the best company Castle could hope for, a trusted friend and advisor, well liked by conservatives and liberals alike, one of the most respected among his fellow Cardinals, and it was easy to see why. He surely had that Irish charm and his lilting Irish brogue made his personality even more affable. It would take more than Mulholland's charm and Castle's power, however, to stop Ferranti, and stop him they must, at any cost.

Ferranti's ideas had always been dangerous and now it could cost the world one of the greatest Popes it would ever see. A man who, like Peter, the first Pope, often appeared to act before he thought, but whom Castle knew well enough to know that this Pope had thought out every move he made with great care, and only after much prayer did John XXIV take action on anything important.

The first order of business they decided that night would be to meet with Brunetti. Once Castle was convinced of Ferranti's treasonous plans, Mulholland knew Castle would take action. But he also knew his friend well enough to know that he still was not totally convinced that Ferranti actually thought he could pull this off.

The next morning found Castle in the Vatican Library. He already knew that Morelli would be at breakfast and that Brunetti always came straight to the library after Mass, preferring to eat a hearty mid-morning meal rather than breakfast. So Castle skipped his own breakfast that day, something he rarely did, believing as Leslie did, that breakfast was the most important meal of the day, but today's task was far more important than Castle's own temporal being. This was the future of the Church at stake.

Brunetti was surprised to have such an early morning visitor; in fact, he had the door still locked, as was his custom, while he sorted through his list of things that needed to be accomplished that day. Most of the Cardinals and other Vatican officials thought the librarians had an easy job—that they just sat there with their dusty old books until someone came in search of something obscure and needed their help to find it. Castle knew differently and respected Brunetti and Morelli and the other librarians for their dedication to the preservation of the books and documents entrusted to their care. He knew that Brunetti personally, as head librarian, scanned the shelves on a daily basis for anything out of place or any books that looked like they needed care, and his ministering to the books were as gentle as those of the kindest nurse caring for the sick and dying. Brunetti loved the library and the Church. He didn't look at all like the stereotypical librarian. He preferred casual clothes to the monk's robe most of the others in his order wore on a daily basis. He wore his robes only for Mass and when he went out in public. In the library, he preferred a pair of khaki pants and Docksiders with a short sleeve knit shirt, keeping his robe on a hanger in his tiny office. Although the library was kept cool to help protect the books, Brunetti often joked about the fact that he was a 'hot-blooded Italian' and couldn't stand a lot of bulky clothes. He almost never wore long sleeves and his muscular build and hairy arms had always made Castle think Brunetti looked more like a longshoreman than a librarian.

"Cardinal Castle," Brunetti greeted him jovially as he unlocked the door, "to what do I owe the honor of this visit so early in the morning?"

"Some important business I am hoping you can help me with," was Castle's no nonsense reply.

"Nothing like getting straight to the point," thought Brunetti.

Brunetti quickly moved aside his daily calendar and invited Castle to sit next to him at the small table in his office. "Coffee?" asked Brunetti.

He always had a small pot of Brazilian coffee brewing in his office this early in the morning. Later on, he would go to the kitchen and have a breakfast of ham and eggs and lots of toast with butter with the Vatican cooks. He much preferred their company to most of those who would be at breakfast in the staff dining room, including Morelli who seemed to aggravate Brunetti more and more lately with his rigid attitude. Morelli had alluded on more than one occasion to those who weren't intelligent or disciplined enough to study for the priesthood and chose the less rigorous religious life instead. Of course, any fool knew that the religious life had far more demands than the priesthood, but Brunetti didn't waste his time trying to argue with Morelli. He knew it was a constant source of irritation to Morelli that he had to report to a brother, not a fellow priest. Brunetti found he really couldn't take Morelli early in the morning, another reason for delaying his breakfast, although he had formed this habit a long time before Morelli came to the library. He had always preferred getting his day in order first and then tackling his tasks one at a time and he received great pleasure from crossing things off his list once accomplished. He now had his list computerized in Outlook, but he still wrote down his list with pen and ink each morning and derived a strange gratification from the scratch of the pen across the paper as he crossed off each 'to do' item as 'done.' He wished he could have been a scribe in the old days, carefully writing down each word of some holy person's prophecy on a scroll, and his favorite part of the library was the special sealed off room that held many of these ancient scrolls.

Now, as Cardinal Castle seated himself at the round oak table, Brunetti relaxed. He was always a bit nervous when one of the Cardinals showed up in his library. It usually meant trouble, since most of the time they sent underlings to do their research. The last Cardinal that came into the library, Ferranti, Brunetti was sure was there to stir up trouble. He knew Ferranti had been coming to Morelli for help and from what Morelli had told him about the research Ferranti was engaged in, it could only mean one thing.

Brunetti didn't really want to think about the meaning of Ferranti's mysterious actions, and right now he didn't want to think about what Castle's visit might mean. He would much rather be delving through the ancient scrolls in the sealed vault than sitting here waiting to hear what Castle wanted. But, Brunetti had a great deal of respect and admiration for Castle. Even Morelli, who hated everything for which Cardinal Castle stood theologically, respected the man for his position and because he was a true gentleman. After Castle had taken a few sips of his coffee, he got right down to it. It was as Brunetti had feared.

"I understand Cardinal Ferranti has been doing some research in the library, with Morelli's assistance," Castle began.

Brunetti, with a nervous cough, replied, "Yes, Cardinal, that is correct."

How much did Castle know already? Surely Morelli hadn't gone to him, even if he was concerned about Ferranti's plot. More likely, Mulholland, in whom Brunetti had confided his fears, had gone to Castle. In fact, as he thought about it, he was certain it was Mulholland. Brunetti now wondered if he had subconsciously gone to Mulholland because he himself wanted to get Castle involved. Brunetti certainly didn't want to see Ferranti succeed, but he would rather not be involved himself in what was going on. The next words out of Castle's mouth stunned Brunetti.

"So, Brother Marcus, what do you think we should do about this?"

Castle was actually asking his advice! Brunetti was speechless. Why would a Cardinal, and the most powerful Cardinal in the Vatican no less, be coming to him for advice? What would he say to the Cardinal and what would the Cardinal do with his advice? A million thoughts ran through Brunetti's mind. He could excuse himself on the pretense of being ill; he could tell the Cardinal he would pray about it and get back to him; he could just faint right here on the floor of his office (he actually felt as thought he might pass out). He knew, however, that Castle would not get up from the table until he answered him.

"Well, Cardinal, I suggest we fight fire with fire. You are an intelligent man, a respected man, a holy man. I think you know already what 'we' must do."

Castle smiled and nodded, "You are right, as usual, Brother Marcus Brunetti; you are a wise man and a tactful man. And, a holy man yourself," he added.

Chapter 15

Carson Valley, Nevada

Leslie's life after the trip to Connecticut had changed forever. She was now hurtling down a path that made her feel like Alice in Wonderland, as she started on her journey by falling into the rabbit hole. Leslie wondered if she was somehow caught in a fantasyland. She wasn't quite certain she was still sane. And yet, it felt so right. She, Fred and Runningwater had held many three-way conversations by teleconference on the plans for the Foundation and for the big event to be held in September. Things were moving along quickly, maybe too quickly. And yet, she sometimes felt it wasn't real. She had also called Sara to fill her in in on the visit to Foxwoods and the plan for the Creation Foundation. She had not mentioned her encounter with the Matriarch; Sara would think she was crazy. As close as the two were, and despite the many things they shared in common, religion was not one of them. Sara was probably an agnostic, but it was a subject they never really discussed much. Leslie had always sensed Sara's uneasiness whenever she brought up the subject of religion and Leslie had never thought it was her job to proselytize, especially to her life-long friend. But one of the things they did share was their love for nature and their concern for the environment, and it was this commonality that prompted Leslie to include Sara in on the planning for this project. Sara was more than enthusiastic. In fact, Leslie wished now that she had included Sara in on the visit to Runningwater. Having her there might have saved her some time in filling her in after the fact, but perhaps even more importantly, Leslie felt that if Sara had been there, she could have diffused some of the electricity that she felt being alone in the room with Runningwater. The man certainly had a powerful effect on her, and she knew the feeling was mutual. Sara was more than willing to tackle this project and contribute anything she could to its success. She had spent many years volunteering for The Nature Conservancy, and for the Hudson Riverkeeper Association, as well as serving on the board of the local Birding Society and she had lots of ideas for fundraising activities that could be done in the casinos. Sara would be her right hand and would work with Fred and Runningwater to bring this project to fruition. Leslie felt an immense relief knowing that she would not need to travel to Connecticut as often as she originally thought she would.

The casino project was keeping Leslie very busy; in fact she had to work well into the nights on the writing projects she had promised her publishers just to keep up with everything. Despite the heavy load of work she was now faced with, the rest of her message from God was haunting her and she knew she had to do something about the other mandates she was given. Bringing Sara into the picture on the project to Honor and Protect God's Creation was the impetus she needed to understand now that she was to be the catalyst for these mandates. Once this plan was in motion, it would take care of itself, and despite the fact that she knew Runningwater wanted more of her involvement, she was able to convince him that this project needed to be run by the Native Americans themselves and that even Fred and Sara should eventually be replaced by Native Americans. Knowing that her role was as the planner and the person with the vision made her sleep a little easier. In fact, it wasn't long before her second mandate was already on its way to being fulfilled, even without her knowledge!

Leslie got the strangest email one afternoon from Tom Barton, a famous software designer, who had heard about the environmental project. Somehow, the plan with the Native American casinos had already gotten out to someone outside the selected circle. As she read his email, she realized that it was probably Joseph Runningwater who talked to Barton, since Barton's company, SoftTech, designed software for the casino industry. Or it could have been Fred who talked with him; she knew SoftTech also designed a lot of programs used by governmental agencies.

Someone had told Barton about the project because his email said he had heard about Leslie's proposal and was intrigued by it. He was planning to fly into Reno the day after tomorrow on business and wanted to meet with her while he was in town. Could she meet him at the steak house inside Harrah's for lunch?! She was ecstatic at the thought that he might want to help fund this project, but she would soon find out this meeting would answer her questions about the second part of the message from the Matriarch.

She dressed carefully for this lunch meeting, pulling out one of her east coast business suits, a navy blue, military-style, wool suit with a short skirt and brass buttoned jacket with epaulets. A gold silk blouse and small gold hoop earrings completed her outfit. She knew that she would recognize Barton from the pictures she had seen on the Internet when she Googled his name. The man was worth billions of dollars. He lived on a ranch just outside Laramie, Wyoming, although he maintained offices in Chicago and Denver. She spent the entire day before her meeting researching Barton and found no great interest in environmental causes. In fact, he had set up a large foundation, but most of its funding went for social justice, with a focus on gay and lesbian issues. She was becoming more and more curious about this meeting.

She arrived about twenty minutes early and decided to let the hostess know she was with the Barton party, get seated the restaurant, and have a cup of tea while she waited. She was still sipping her tea when she spotted Barton, walking towards her with another man, whom he later introduced as the head of his foundation, Richard Steel. At first she thought the two might be lovers, but their demeanor at lunch was purely business and she decided she had been wrong in her initial reaction. As the waiter took their order, Leslie was tempted to order a glass of wine to take the edge of her nervousness, but she wanted to be at her sharpest during their discussion. Steel ordered a glass of Chardonnay but Barton stuck with sparkling water as did Leslie. All three ordered large salads with grilled salmon and once the order was taken, Barton got right down to business. This lunch was starting to remind Leslie of her meeting with Runningwater, except that now she was on the opposite side of the table. She had no idea what was in the leather folder that Steel had placed on the table beside his water glass.

Steel was quiet during lunch as Barton told Leslie about his company, the various software systems they had designed, and about his foundation. Like many of the venture philanthropists who had emerged from the technology world, he had his own ideas about how he would invest his money in social change. Leslie knew a great deal about Barton's philanthropic interests from the research she had done the previous day and a half. He was openly gay and much of his money went to fund LGBT causes, particularly youth centers. He had also given millions to various social issues, including education and research on AIDS, social justice agencies and minority scholarships. But what he had heard from his client, Runningwater, had started him thinking.

"After talking with Runningwater," he began to explain to Leslie, "I realized that while funding scholarships, housing programs and all the things in which I've been investing in the past, there is still something missing in my philanthropic endeavors. To really stop social injustice, we need to address the cause of this injustice. Hatred and bigotry can only end if humankind begins to understand and appreciate the differences in each of us. I've thought long and hard about how this could happen, but it will take more money than my foundation has."

It was then that Steel cleared his throat and offered the leather folder to Leslie, explaining that it contained a plan on which they wanted her advice. Barton wanted Leslie's advice! It was unbelievable. But an even bigger shock was in store. As Leslie opened the folder, there on page one was the Barton Foundation logo and four words in large black type, "Recognize and Celebrate Diversity." Leslie was so stunned she trembled as she turned the page to see what else was in this thick folder; she felt she had seen her future. She knew then that whatever it was this man wanted from her, it was his. She glanced at Barton and he looked puzzled by Leslie's reaction; was she not open to this idea? Was she somehow offended?

"Let me explain my plan," Barton said eagerly, bringing her out of her state of shock. "You see, after talking with Runningwater, I realized you were the one person who would have the vision to help me see this thing through. I've been contributing millions of dollars to housing programs, debt counseling, work programs, all designed to get the underserved populations of this country into a stronger position to help themselves. I've poured tons of money into helping young gays, lesbians, and transgendered people find themselves and learn how to deal with their differentness. However, about a year ago, I realized that no matter what I tried to do to improve their state of life, they were still being held back by bigotry, prejudice and the hatred of people who didn't understand the fact that all our differences should make us a stronger people, not a world torn apart. It became clear to me that I needed to do something to get at the root of the problem. I have a younger brother who is in the marines and has served tours of duty in Pakistan, Iraq and Afghanistan. When he came back from his last stint over there, we talked for hours about how the Middle East has always been in turmoil, but the question that kept bothering me throughout the conversation was why these people hate Americans so much. He explained to me that these men grew up in schools of hate. They were taught from an early age to hate Christians, and especially Americans, and to do whatever they could to destroy them. They had corrupted the Muslim religion from one that revered peace and harmony as their holy people taught, into a twisted corruption of their faith that destroyed anything that was different from their way of thinking.

I found it difficult to understand why people of three religions, all claiming a common father in Abraham, could not get along with each other. This got me thinking that if people could be trained at an early age to hate and destroy, they could be taught to love and build up one another. And so my plan was born. What you have in this folder is a plan for a new society, starting in the United States, but eventually spreading to the whole planet.

First, I want to start schools that will focus on teaching our young people from pre-school age to high school to recognize and celebrate the diversity that is their gift. And it won't end with the schools; it needs to permeate their every waking moment. We know that most kids learn their values from their parents and when parents are bigoted, prejudiced and hateful they will pass these traits along to their children. But we can influence every other part of their lives, and that is no small feat. The schools have them for six hours a day and that is a good start, but what do these kids do after school? They lose themselves in an electronic world and that is where I, and others like me, come in. My software designers have already completed Phase I of a whole new generation of video games, ones that have no violence or destruction but games that revolve around a group of teens working together to build up a city that has been destroyed. They learn from each other that each has a different skill and talent based on their diverse backgrounds, and that only by working together can they save their city. Another game uses a similar theme to rebuild a destroyed planet. Phase one has twenty-seven games in all. Now, I know that you are thinking the kids will never buy these games. But we have already tested the concept with a group of innovators. Are you familiar with the concept of innovators, early adopters, etc?"

Leslie was familiar with this concept because she had studied it in a marketing class and understood what Barton planned to target those innovators, the leaders who would influence others.

Barton continued, "In his book, *The Tipping Point*, Malcolm Gladwell, discusses a similar theory that involves Mavens, Connectors and Salespeople. But, basically there are leaders in any group, and then there are those who get in on any new concept early on, and there are the followers who will reluctantly jump in because 'everyone else is doing it.' Then of course there are those stubborn few who will never change, no matter how exciting any new innovation is. These are the lost ones that you don't even try to convert. We have targeted the leaders—the innovators and the early adopters—who will influence the followers. We've held focus groups with these young leaders to see what it would take to move them from the violent video games they're currently playing into this new generation of entertainment. We have the programs that will do it. We know, also, that the more they play these games, the more likely that their real life behavior will be patterned after those games. We've seen the negative effects of this patterning in the number of homicides involving kids emulating a game they've played, and we know that for some young people separating fantasy from reality becomes harder and harder. If we can get them playing games that involve recognizing and celebrating their diversity, it won't be long before their real life behavior emulates this fantasy world. But it won't stop with video games; we will target the movie and television industry as well. It will take a little time and a great deal of money to do this, but we have the solution laid out in our plan."

Before Leslie could ask the question that was burning in her mind, Barton answered it.

"I am sure you are wondering how all of this involves you and why I asked you to meet me today. As you read through this plan, you will begin to understand the magnitude of this project and how it will influence the thinking and behavior of the next generation. And, here is where you come in. Runningwater is a good client of mine and he naturally approached me to help with this environmental project he is working on with you. He also told me it was all your idea and that he agreed to this partly because of your own passion for this idea. I was amazed when he shared your proposal with me, because I had already had a similar idea. Frankly, you will see when you read through my proposal tonight that it is very similar to your own proposal to Runningwater, because, quite honestly, I lifted many of your own ideas to incorporate into my plan. You see, we're both working on the same plan—to save our environment. While you and Runningwater are working on solutions for the catastrophe facing our physical environment, I am working on saving our social environment. We compliment each other quite nicely."

Leslie was back at the Ancient Bristlecone Forest for a moment, listening to her mandate from God— "Honor and protect My Creation,

Recognize and celebrate the Diversity I birthed from My Womb, Return My Church to the Prophets and Mystics." Suddenly, in a matter of weeks, it seemed she had the answers to at least two of these questions that had haunted her from the moment she began to descend that mountain. She wondered if she might actually have the answers to all three. Could Runningwater and Barton be the prophets and mystics God had talked to her about? Although she hadn't discussed religion with either of them, she somehow sensed that Runningwater was a deeply spiritual man, but she picked up nothing close to this spirituality in Barton. And she didn't think either of them would welcome any connection with the hierarchy of the Church. She still wasn't sure what Barton wanted from her. But again, he answered her question before she asked it.

"The reason I need you, is to help me sell this idea to others in my industry.

This plan will take a lot of funding, and I am intrigued by the way you and Runningwater have come up with a plan to finance your project. The gaming industry is already buzzing about what Runningwater is up to, with his big 'Pow Wow' as they are calling it. I need to create that buzz in the technology and entertainment industry. I already have the foundation in place to fund the early phase of this project, but we will need a lot more than that. I want you to help me develop a plan for getting every software designer, every record company, every production company, every movie mogul in Hollywood, and every entertainer behind this. We need to come up with a plan to raise the kind of money that will make this thing happen. And I believe everyone in this industry will support it when they hear our case. First, because many people in this industry are part of a minority in one way or another. Second, because these people can smell a profit a mile away and they know that converting everything we already have in place will mean big bucks for them in the long run. There will be more video games to sell, more media on which to play these games, more music to sell, more movies and television shows to promote. They will come out of this with a great return on their investment. But I need your help to put that structure together. You don't have to answer right now, but take this folder home and read it, I will call you tomorrow evening and we can talk more and perhaps set up a time when you can come to Laramie or to Denver where we can plan our next steps."

Steel, who had had been quiet but nodding in agreement at all of Barton's statements, now took over. He pulled out his and Barton's business cards with their private cell numbers and email addresses and handed them to Leslie, entered all of Leslie's information into his iPhone, and scheduled a time for their conference call tomorrow evening, being careful to coordinate time zone changes.

As they said their goodbyes at the valet parking area, Leslie breathed a deep sigh. Climbing into her X Terra, she was tempted to pull into a parking space and read the entire folder right then and there, but she opted for driving home, changing into her pajamas and slippers, starting a fire and settling down in front of the fireplace with a large mug of green tea, a dark chololate bar, a bowl of strawberries, and Barton's plan.

The plan really didn't hold many surprises; Barton had explained it very well. She was, however, surprised by the detail in the proposal, as surprised as Runningwater had seemed at hers. It was interesting being on the other side of this process, and Leslie said a prayer of thanksgiving that she had not had to develop another complete plan. But she kept thinking about Barton's words—that they were all working on the same plan, and indeed it did seem that there was a Divine Plan at work, although not one of the people involved had uttered those words. Her mind kept going back to that cover page and she turned and stared at it at least eight times as she read through the proposal. Could it be that Barton, and perhaps Runningwater too, had had similar revelations, maybe not through the Matriarch, but through some other medium, and that they were all part of this Divine Scheme, part of a new Salvation History?

Chapter 16

Vatican City

The Council was about to begin. Tomorrow morning, the Cardinals would start to arrive from all over the world. Those from Italy and the rest of Europe would be the first to arrive. Most of the others would arrive sometime that evening and those who were there in time for dinner would gather in small groups, usually those who were politically aligned with each other, but occasionally by country of origin. Castle had planned to have dinner with two of the American Cardinals, Edward Mannion of New York, and Carlos Fernandez, one of the newest Cardinals from Houston which was becoming one of the fastest growing cities in the United States, along with his friend Mulholland, another Irish Cardinal, Sean Connors, the Korean Kim Chung Lee, the Italian Gilberto Romano and Baharta Brahatta of South Africa. They were all key players who shared a concern that Ferranti and his cohorts were out of hand and had to be stopped. They would use the hours spent over dinner and brandies to plan their strategy. Each of them had been working behind the scenes over the past month, since getting the email from Castle that their help was needed, and Mannion, Romano and Brahatta had actually arrived five days earlier on the pretext of using these final days to prepare the papers they would be presenting, but in actuality they had spent most of those five days conferring with Castle and Mulholland. Pope John XXIV had been consulted by phone several times as well.

John had been more than shocked when he heard of Ferranti's scheme and at first refused to believe Castle when he revealed the plot to overthrow the Pope. John had always thought the best of everyone, even those who considered themselves his enemies. He refused to believe that even Ferranti would come up with this evil plan, until Castle had shown him the proof just before he left for his retreat. Castle and Brunetti had been able to secure notes from Ferranti's research, copies of emails sent to several Cardinals and an actual copy of the paper he would present at the Council. How they had obtained these documents, the Pope did not ask. He really did not want to know, and he trusted Castle's integrity enough to not doubt that he was acting in the best interest of the Church. John had known this would be a difficult Council when he planned it. This gathering of the Cardinals would shape the future of the Church more than any other in recent history. The changes would be even more sweeping and more controversial than those of Vatican II. In addition to seeking confirmation of his AIDS plan in which the Church would invest billions of dollars, John XXIV was proposing that the Church accept marriage as an option for the clergy, and that women be admitted into the priesthood. He knew these changes would not come easy for many of the Cardinals and he had no idea of whether he would be successful, but now was certainly the time for someone to open the door for serious discussion. Castle had been working diligently on building enough support for the Pope's proposed changes and felt that the AIDS plan and the rescinding of the celibacy requirement for priests would be accepted, although he doubted that there was enough support for the ordination of women. That would likely be years away, but the fact that this Pope was willing to open the subject up for serious discussion was in itself a monumental milestone for the Church.

Castle had completed his research on the early church's decision to impose celibacy on its priests, after several hundred years of married clergy, and prepared an impressive document that would be proposed to the Cardinals. The role of women in the Church had also been addressed in great detail, citing the role of early female Disciples of Christ. But, after taking the pulse of the Cardinals as best he could, he was certain they would not go as far as to accept women priests. The AIDS pandemic was rampant in almost every part of the world and most of the Cardinals knew that something had to be done. A slim majority, but enough to carry the vote, was supportive of John's plan. The Americans especially supported the removal of the celibacy requirement, having had their share of headaches dealing with the pedophilia scandals that had bankrupted several archdioceses and caused a dramatic loss of parishioners and funding in many others. They felt their people were more than ready for married priests, but even they, with all their talk of equality, were reluctant to accept women into their world.

John XXIV, however, was not prepared for the backlash this Council had caused. He knew that Ferranti would lead the charge to preserve the Church as it was, but had never suspected he would go as far as he apparently had. Although none of them were sure exactly how he would propose to oust John XXIV, they did accept the reality that this was Ferranti's ultimate goal. Their best guess was that he would first attempt to defeat the Pope's proposal mandating the changes, and then would use his victory to attack the Pope personally, claiming that John's goal was to destroy the Church. Once Ferranti had the ear of the assembly, they were certain he would pull out all the stops. They knew he was already trying to build allies from among those Cardinals who were on the fence as far as John XXIV's papacy went.

Ferranti had presented his case for keeping the Vatican out of the AIDS issue and maintaining a celibate male priesthood to just about every member of the College of Cardinals, even those he knew would side with John XXIV on this issue. He had only revealed his plot to overthrow the Pope to a few select people, those whom he knew would side with him and who had the power to influence others. He felt that once he had won victory on these three issues, the ousting of the Pope would follow soon after.

Castle's dinner companions that evening were all happy to see each other and greeted each other with warm embraces. As happy as they were to be together with their brother Cardinals, they were all concerned about this threat to the Pope, more concerned than they would have been if they had felt the Holy Father's life had been threatened. Popes had had their lives threatened before and John Paul II had been shot, but this was a more grievous threat, an actual assault on John XXIV's character, his dedication to the Church and his ability to fill the shoes of Peter. They each knew as they gathered for dinner, that this evening could decide the fate of the Church they loved so dearly.

During dinner, they caught up with each other and what was happening in each of their countries and in their personal lives. They waited until they had finished the crème brulee, topped with fresh raspberries, one of the few desserts George occasionally allowed himself to indulge in, and adjourned to George's suite for coffee and brandy to get down to business. George had copies of the documents he had shared with the Pope for each of them and summarized the problem in about twenty minutes. In addition, he had a computer generated list of all the Cardinals which he had coded *PJ*, for supporters of the Pope's position, *CF* for those whom he was certain would support Ferranti, and *UN* for those who he considered undecided, or neutral. The eight men discussed the *PJ* list and concurred that almost all of these were assuredly in the Pope's camp. Two were moved to the *UN* column after Lee and Mulholland had divulged some recent conversations that indicated these two might possibly be swayed by Ferranti. Next they reviewed the column of those who were believed to be staunch supporters of Ferranti and would be certain to vote with him on any issues that came before the Council. This list, the group felt certain was accurate and they made no changes to it. The next list, unfortunately, was the largest and the one that would decide the fate of the Pope and the Church. This list would take several hours of discussion and a fresh pot of coffee, along with a plate of fruit and cheese. While they waited for the refreshments, most of the men excused themselves for a trip to the rest room, Connors had been barely able to contain himself through the coffee and brandy due to his enlarged prostate condition. Lee and Castle both were accustomed to a daily walk and the two of them took a 15-minute walk together. Castle had always admired Lee and the more he worked with the man, the more impressed he was with his style. He was a no-nonsense man, and to many he seemed a bit too blunt and uncommunicative. Lee had always been overly sensitive about his poor command of English and Italian and the more nervous he was, the more he tended to stutter and stumble over English, especially. He could hold his own in Italian although he was certainly not as fluent as Castle. Knowing of Lee's discomfort with English, Castle always conversed with him in Italian when they were alone and for this Lee was eternally grateful. He had managed to participate in the conversation quite well when all eight men were together, but he was always more nervous when conversing one-on-one with English speaking people. Castle thanked Lee for his work in helping to organize the Council. If there was one thing Lee excelled at, it was organizing and planning. Castle touched Lee's arm as he spoke.

"I hope you know how much I appreciate your help with this Council, Kim. You are a key part of the Holy Father's strategy and he joins me in also thanking you for your work on the AIDS project in Asia."

Lee, embarrassed at this show of affection and appreciation, stumbled even in Italian, "Gracia, Cardinal Castle, it is always good to be appreciated for what you do and I am always happy to be of service to the Holy Father."

Castle's face grew dark for a moment, "You are aware that this Council is the most important milestone in the Church's recent history." It was a statement, not a question, although Lee answered it as though Castle was asking his opinion.

"Of course, and we will all be remembered for this, no matter what the outcome."

Castle shook his head in agreement. "You are so right, Cardinal Lee. Let us hope that history will be kind to us. What do you think our chances for success are?"

Castle held his breath, for he knew that although Mannion, Connors and Fernandez were the eternal optimists and would also say what they thought Castle wanted to hear, Lee was his Nathaniel, a man without guile, who would speak the truth.

"I think we will be successful with the AIDS plan and the celibacy issue and if we are, Ferranti's plan will end before he has a chance to put it in motion. But it will be a long, hard fight and there will be much bitterness to deal with, and much healing will be needed after this Council is over."

They were back inside Castle's suite by this time, the cool evening air having cleared their minds and refreshed their bodies.

"Cardinal Lee, I am glad you enjoy walking as much as I do. I needed this time with you."

As the eight men settled down to fresh coffee, sparkling water, and a grand assortment of cheeses and fruits—mangoes, grapes and huge sweet strawberries on a large sliver tray, they each got the lists out of their pockets, having been sure to keep these lists on their persons at all time. One never knew where and when Ferranti's spies would work their way—even into Castle's suite. Connors' list was crumpled and had coffee stains on it already, but Castle was certain he would guard it with his life. Even though Connors tended to be a rather messy man, he was well aware that this information must not fall into the wrong hands.

Castle asked Lee to read the names of those Cardinals that had the *UN* mark in the column after their name. Next to this column was a blank column, which would be used to fill in one of the eight names of the men around the table, the man who would talk with each undecided Cardinal and try to get a feel for his position. Once that work was done, and it would have to be done in the next two days, they would meet again for dinner and determine which of the Cardinals they needed to meet with in order to try and sway them to the Pope's side. Lee accepted the task of being the recorder and the moderator for this discussion with an enthusiasm he rarely showed in public. The process of getting through the list took two hours and there was much discussion over some of the names, even a heated debate on a few of them. But in the end, they had moved seven names to the *PJ* column and three to the *CF* column, leaving forty-seven undecided names to be contacted over the next two days. They spent another hour assigning each of the forty-seven to one of the eight men gathered on this fateful evening. They carefully assigned the right man for each of the forty-seven, the one who had the best chance of getting the reluctant Cardinals to discuss their leanings on these issues. They established a time to meet the evening after next, this time in Mulholland's suite, hoping to avoid anyone noticing the fact that these eight were conspiring to thwart Ferranti's plans.

Each man left the room knowing they would have a great task ahead of them. Some of the visits needed to be done by phone, but most of them would be done in person as the Cardinals gathered in Rome. None of them were eager to do any of these meetings by phone; they wanted to meet personally with their assigned 'prospects,' mainly because they wanted to impress upon the neutral Cardinals the importance of this meeting, and so they could read body language and facial expression, but also because there was no assurance that Ferranti had not tapped into phone lines within the Vatican. It was agreed that if any of the visits must be done by phone, they would use their cell phones.

Chapter 17

Laramie, Wyoming

As Leslie stepped off the private jet Barton had sent to pick her up in Reno, she was surprised to see Barton himself driving the red Ferrari parked on the tarmac. She had expected he would send Steel or perhaps one of his underlings to pick her up.

"I have a surprise for you, Leslie," Barton greeted her.

It was an odd way to start a conversation, thought Leslie, but Barton was not known for using words needlessly; he generally got right to the point.

"A surprise? Is it bigger than a breadbox?" joked Leslie.

"Much bigger!" Barton laughed.

They climbed into the Ferrari and headed towards Barton's ranch. Leslie would soon find out that Barton actually had three surprises, each considerably larger than a breadbox. The first one was that they were going horseback riding while they talked business, and Barton had secured for her a horse that looked amazingly like her own Mancha. His own horse was a black stallion named Lancelot, and Barton proved to be an excellent horseman. While they rode, he told Leslie that he had reviewed the changes she had made to his project proposal and was pleased with the details she was able to fill in. Her plan to use his commitment as a challenge to the rest of the technology companies and members of the entertainment industry was perfectly outlined and he was certain it would be a success. Leslie had added the details that were needed before he could present his proposal to his peers. He had completed the reports on the focus groups and had identified a list of targeted companies with whom he had appointments scheduled over the next three weeks. It was easy for Barton to schedule appointments with the leaders in the industry; he was well respected and powerful, a person to whom very few people ever said no. What he wanted now was for Leslie to give him some advice on making his presentation to the others.

She had initially wondered how they could have a business meeting while riding, but it was natural for them to talk strategy while riding. They both did their best thinking while on horseback. After about two hours, they headed back to the ranch for a quick shower and change of clothes before lunch. Leslie wasn't sure what the rest of the day would hold, but she was glad she had brought along a dressier outfit. She somehow was pretty certain that lunch would bring more surprises, and she was right. As she came downstairs, dressed in a white cashmere sweater and a pair of black slacks, she was greeted by Barton who was arm in arm with a strikingly handsome young man, obviously his lover. So the second surprise was also bigger than a breadbox, and probably never ate bread. He was slim and trim and looked as though he could be a model, an underwear model, Leslie suspected.

As they sat down to lunch, she found out that Brett Henderson was not an underwear model at all; she had been way off base. He was an accountant, in fact had been Barton's accountant until they became lovers, at which time he turned over the SoftTech account to his business partner, a sharp young woman whom Brett had met while in college. She was right about one thing, though, Brett never ate bread. In fact, he was what some people would call a 'health nut' and Leslie immediately resonated with his love for organic, healthy food. Barton, although not particularly fussy about his eating habits, respected both Brett's and Leslie's preferences and had ordered a light but hearty lunch with lots of protein and virtually no carbohydrates. They had a tossed salad of arugula with avocado and sprouts and grilled chicken, a bowl of fresh fruit for dessert, and freshly brewed herbal tea.

Leslie was enchanted with Brett; he was such a charming and intelligent man, it was easy to see how Barton had fallen in love with him. And Brett would be a perfect addition to this team. Brett could handle the Diversity Peace Fund of the Barton Foundation as Fred was handling the Creation Foundation. In fact, the parallels were amazing. After lunch, the three of them planned the strategy for investing the fund's money and finalized the plan for the start up of the Peace Schools, which would run simultaneously with the introduction of the New Universe video games.

Around 4:30 in the afternoon, Barton said he needed to excuse himself to make a few phone calls and run an errand, but suggested that Brett and Leslie take a break before they would all go out for dinner. He had a favorite place he planned to take them. Brett said Leslie would enjoy it and explained that it was real cowboy place—their specialties included ribs, steaks and prime rib, which made both Leslie and Brett just about gag at the thought, but Brett assured her they made a special western style grilled salmon that was to die for. She and Brett brewed some chamomile tea and sat in the rustic farm kitchen snacking on apple slices with cinnamon and some raw, unsalted almonds. They shared childhood stories; found out that they were both from New York State, although Brett had been a 'Big Apple' resident while Leslie grew up in Albany. Both had fond memories of the Empire State, although neither of them missed the cold weather. Of course, it could get cold in northern Nevada and certainly in Denver, where Brett lived when he wasn't here in Laramie with Barton, but it wasn't anything like the bitter, damp cold of New York.

Leslie found herself telling Brett all about Michael and about her family, while Brett shared with Leslie that he had also been married once and had a son whom he rarely saw until recently. He had married very young, perhaps in an effort to convince himself that he was a 'normal,' heterosexual young man. The marriage didn't last long. When his wife found out he was gay, she immediately filed for divorce and succeeded in denying him visiting rights with their son. Years later, his son looked him up and they now saw each other about every other month, although they could never regain the father-son relationship that had been taken away from them by the court system and a bitter woman.

Jason, Brett's son, had no problem with the fact that his father was gay, despite the bitterness toward Brett that his mother tried to impart on him as he was growing up. Jason was now a mature young man, who understood that homosexuality was not a crime, a sin, or a disease, but an orientation with which people were born. Although he could never fully understand his father's world, he accepted it and Barton without question and even tried to convince his mother that Brett and Barton were a good influence on him. He was interested in graphic design and Barton had promised him a job in his company as soon as he finished college.

While Leslie and Brett stood side by side at the sink, cleaning up their dishes, Barton called and said he was delayed for about half hour and that he would meet Leslie and Brett at the restaurant. Leslie excused herself, went to freshen up for dinner, and grabbed her leather jacket since the air had grown cool. Brett was waiting at the door when she bounced down the stairs, eager to see more of Laramie. Brett was driving a Porsche convertible that suited his look perfectly; it was a deep blue, almost the exact color of his eyes. Leslie climbed into the passenger seat and fastened her seat belt. He put the top up since the sun had set, knowing how cold those Wyoming nights could get. On the drive, Leslie and Brett talked about how ironic it was that Barton's ranch was so close in proximity to that fateful scene of one of the worst hate crimes in the country, the fence where a young gay man had been tied and beaten to death. Leslie recalled seeing *The Laramie Project* in a summer theater production in Hartford and what a profound effect it had had on her and Michael. Barton, Brett told her, likewise had been affected by the actual incident and it was, in fact, the impetus for him starting his foundation.

Brett was eager to show Leslie their town.

"I hope you are staying long enough to get the real tour and see more of Laramie," he said, flashing those teeth which were white enough to blind a person.

She had a momentary flashback to Joseph Runningwater, remembering his brilliant, full-toothed, white smile. Leslie had originally planned to fly back to Reno tomorrow but she, too, wished she could spend a little more time there. Of course, there would probably be another trip and perhaps that one could be longer.

"No, I really must get back to Nevada tomorrow. I only packed enough for one night and my horses get testy if I'm gone too long."

She still had a lot of things to do to prepare for the big Pow Wow in Connecticut in September. It was like planning a wedding. You think there is so much time, and then all of a sudden, it is upon you and you're caught up in all the last minute details. Leslie didn't like last minute surprises and was determined to have everything in place by the end of June.

"Well, we do have stores in Laramie. You could always buy some extra clothes, but I know what you mean about the horses. My cats literally pull out their own hair if I leave them for more than three days."

It turned out the restaurant, or more accurately the neighborhood bar, wasn't far from the ranch, so it was a short drive. As they stepped inside the door, Leslie thought this must be what they were talking about in the country songs when they sang about a honky tonk. The place was filled with real cowboys though and she felt right at home, despite the country music blaring from the jukebox. She had never been a fan of country music, as much as she loved the old west and cowboys. She liked some of the 'old-timers' like Willie Nelson, Merle Haggard and Dolly Parton but thought that today's country music was more like rock music. She longed for the old Texas Swing she remembered as young girl, the music she always pictured the real cowboys playing around their campfires at night.

She had been in places like this before, the kind of little, unknown dive that had the best food in town, far exceeding the gourmet restaurants written up in all the tourist magazines. In fact she always sought out these kinds of places to write about in her travel stories, so she was thrilled with Barton's choice for their evening meal. It reminded her of a similar spot she and Michael had found once on a drive through Vermont where they had the greatest barbequed chicken she had ever eaten. The hostess showed Brett immediately to a booth in the corner, obviously Barton and Brett's favorite spot. The leather booths had tall backs so she couldn't see if Barton was already seated or not, but as they got closer to the booth, she had her third and final surprise of the day.

Barton was standing up to greet them, but also rising from his corner of the booth was Joseph Runningwater! Leslie was dumbfounded; what on earth was he doing in Laramie? As he embraced her, she remembered that musky cologne and all of a sudden the poem he had given her flashed through her mind in its entirety. Runningwater allowed Leslie to slide into the circular booth next to Brett, while he and Barton took the outside seats. Once Leslie recovered from the shock of seeing Runningwater, it started to make sense. Barton had made it clear from the start that Runningwater had called him asking for his financial support of the Creation Foundation, and had also indicated that Runningwater was a good client of his. Leslie also remembered Runningwater saying on his brief trip to Reno that he had a friend in Wyoming that he wanted to talk with, as well as some Native American casino owners. It all made sense to Leslie now, Runningwater had approached Barton for help, but Barton had his own ideas. And Runningwater didn't mind that he would not have Barton's money for his own project. In fact, he seemed just as motivated by Barton's scheme as he was by his own project.

It dawned on Leslie that the four people sitting in a booth in this out of the way 'honky tonk' would be setting the wheels in motion for a plan that would significantly affect the world. Leslie was in a dream-like state as she thought of how far she had already come since that trip to The Matriarch, but knowing how far she still had to go. She thought again of those three mandates and realized that two of them were closer to reality than she could imagine. But always in the back of her mind was that third message from Yahweh—"Return My Church to the Mystics and Prophets." She still had no idea how that would happen, but after tonight, she was convinced it would.

They had a marvelous dinner and Leslie and Brett even danced to a couple of songs. Neither Barton nor Runningwater were much for dancing and Leslie hadn't danced in years, but Brett was eager to get her onto the floor so she agreed. She couldn't remember when she had had so much fun, possibly not since Michael died. And, between laughter, good food, music and stories about the casino industry, the accounting business and technology, they actually managed to conduct a good deal of business. Barton wanted to know all about the event Runningwater was planning in September and was hoping that Leslie could help him plan something equally as spectacular. He already had the date for the Foxwoods event in his Blackberry and planned to fill a table of ten with Brett, his best software designers, and key marketing people. Leslie wanted to help him, but knew she couldn't tackle this thing right now, with all the other things on her plate. She still had to keep up her writing assignments; otherwise, they would find other writers to take her place, and she wanted to continue her work after these events were over. Although she was beginning to think that this was her life now, and that she might need to think about giving up her writing.

"I think the next step is for you to find someone to organize your event and then we can get together with Sara, who is working with Runningwater's event-planning staff on the details," she offered.

"I wasn't expecting you to personally run the event, but I really intended to use this evening to brainstorm with all of you on what we should do, you know the usual inquiring reporter questions—who, what where, when and how. We already know 'why!' I think I can handle the 'who.' It won't be difficult to get an invitation list together. I already know pretty much who I need to have there. And as to the 'when,' I think it should be soon after the Foxwoods' event, but not too soon. We don't want to get our invitation out until your event is over, Joe."

She had not heard anyone called Runningwater, Joe before, and thought that if it were anyone else, Runningwater would not have welcomed this familiarity.

"Now the 'where' and the 'what' are the big steps. The 'how' we will leave to the person we select do be the coordinator."

They spent a good hour brainstorming different ideas about the where and the what. The two issues were interdependent. They talked about a huge western-themed Bar B Q at Barton's Ranch, a sumptuous gala at the Exploratorium in San Francisco, a bash at the Mile High Stadium in Denver, and a star-studded event in Las Vegas. All of these ideas had merit and each had its own pros and cons. They finally decided on a unique setting, but one that would really impress on people the need for this project.

Chapter 18

Vatican City

The octet of Cardinals had completed their work in the allotted two days. As they gathered in Mulholland's suite, there was an air of hopeful excitement and yet somber overtones permeated the air. The eight men gathered around the fireplace in Mulholland's sitting room after dinner. Each knew that this was the most important task with which they had ever been entrusted. While they were pleased with the work that had been accomplished over the past two days, they recognized, Castle more than any of them, that if they failed in their mission over the next three days the Church as they knew it could be doomed to extinction. They truly believed that if Ferranti had his way, another schism would tear the church asunder and this time, the chasm might not be breached as it had been in the past. The Korean hadn't even waited until dinner was over to push them on to work. Kim Lee, in his usual no-nonsense manner, had opened his folder during dinner, pushing aside his plates and wine glass. He was too nervous, too excited to enjoy his dinner and besides, he had never really adjusted to the rich Italian or French cuisine served at most of the Vatican dinners. He much preferred the simple Korean food of his homeland. As he had dined on the rich French cuisine two nights ago, he had longed for a simple fish and rice dinner, one that just a few years ago would have been a sumptuous meal for him. He had taken his assignment from Castle most seriously. Before the pasta course was finished, he opened the small leather folder he had kept in his hands from the moment he had entered the room, laying it aside only to have a few spoonfuls of soup and to pick at his antipasto and the angel hair pasta in Alfredo sauce. He was anxious to get this tally over with.

Clearing his throat, he began, "My brothers, it seems we've all completed our task in the brief time allotted, and for this I thank you and commend each of you for your dedication to the Holy Father. I would like to go through the list while we finish our dinner so that we can then adjourn to the task of assigning the next round of calls during our after-dinner drinks."

The men listened respectfully, even though Lee was one of the youngest men around the table and, along with Fernandez, one of the newest Cardinals. They respected him for his intelligence and his dedication to the Church, but perhaps even more so for the political persecution he had suffered at the hands of his country's leaders. From his early days as a priest and Bishop, he had spoken out in favor of peace and had suffered the consequences, having been jailed, tortured and removed from his office as Bishop under his country's previous regime. It was a blessing for the Church when he was finally, under the new South Korean democracy, released from prison and elevated to the position of Cardinal. John XXIV counted Lee as one of his dearest friends and trusted advisors, and he admired the man tremendously.

Now, Lee went through the list of the Cardinals one by one as the rest of them enjoyed their meal, stopping long enough to enjoy just a few bites of the wonderful Alaskan halibut encrusted with macadamia nuts Mulholland had ordered for them. Romano and Mulholland, the gourmets of the group, enjoyed every morsel of the food and both wished Lee had waited until after dinner to get to work, but they admired him enough to tolerate this interruption of their dinner. And all of the men knew it would be a long night and long couple of days ahead of them, so they knew Lee was right to get started as soon as possible. Lee pulled out a small, slender, black pen, a gift from his mother on the day he had left his small village for the seminary, and began reading the names off, beginning with Alberti, from Sicily. As each name was read off, the man who had been assigned to contact him reported the results, and Lee made a note on his list as to whether the Cardinal in question should be moved to the *CF* or the *PJ* column, or remain in the *UN* column. The results were encouraging. Of the forty-seven names in the undecided column, they were confident that twelve of them could be moved to the *PJ* column, and just four of them were definitely in Ferranti's camp and so were moved to the *CF* column. There were now just thirty-one names still undecided and after dinner, the men would discuss who should call on these thirty-one to try to sway their allegiance to the Pope's plan. After these assignments were made, they would review the list of Ferranti's supporters and decide if any of them might be swayed to change their vote, and if so, these would also be assigned. They had also discussed during dinner several names of other Cardinals who might help them with their task if needed. These included Stanley Wallace of Australia,

Raoul Perez of Mexico, Luis Bastiani of Argentina and Peter Van Leuk of The Netherlands. Each of these they felt could be entrusted with this important task, although they were reluctant to bring too many others into their circle. There was some debate about whether they should keep it to the original eight, or perhaps bring the number to an even dozen. There was certainly precedent for having a group of twelve who would proselytize to the world!

When dinner was complete and Romano had cleaned the remaining sauce off his plate with a piece of that wonderful bread for which the Vatican Bakery was known, they all rose and headed into the sitting room. Mulholland had quite a lovely art gallery in his sitting room and Brahatta and Mannion spent some time admiring the Botticelli's and Caravaggio's on the wall before sitting down to coffee and after-dinner cordials. Although Castle would have enjoyed another after dinner walk, he sensed that this evening Lee was eager to complete their task and so he regretfully gave up his usual after-dinner stroll around the grounds. Romano, Fernandez and Connors had excused themselves for a rest room break, giving Mulholland an opportunity to discuss his artwork with its admirers. One of the benefits of having a suite in the Vatican was that you were allowed to choose several pieces of art from the storage rooms of the Vatican Museum and display it in your rooms for as long as you liked, and rotate it as often as you liked with anything else not on display in the public areas of the Museum. Mulholland was one of the few who kept the Museum preparators busy rotating the artwork on a regular basis. Most of the Cardinals assigned to the Vatican and other employees either picked out a few favorites and stuck with them for their tenure in the Vatican, or just kept the artwork that their suite's previous occupants had selected, not knowing enough about art, or perhaps not caring enough about it, to take the time to wander though the storage rooms with a museum curator, most of whom used these tours as an opportunity to insure that the Cardinals in question were adequately made aware of the curator's superior knowledge of art.

When the rest of the men returned from the men's room, the group once again gathered over coffee, tea and after-dinner drinks. Tonight, they would skip the fruit and cheese, having had such a filling meal already. If the meeting went into the wee hours of the morning, Mulholland had arranged to have a light breakfast brought in, scrambled eggs, juice, fresh fruit, strong coffee and biscotti. Lee took the seat in front of the fireplace where he could see everyone clearly.

In his early boyhood, he had wanted to be a teacher, and he now assumed the role of the head of the class, leading his students through the exercise. He was a natural born facilitator, respectful of his 'students' but clearly in charge. As he went through the names, many of the men who had made the initial call felt comfortable enough to also make the next visit to the Cardinals they had spoken to, although there were several that were the cause of a lengthy discussion on who could best influence these men. After two of these lengthy discussions, Lee wisely suggested that they list those who were an easy decision first, and defer the 'tough ones' for further discussion. Once this was decided, the initial assignments went rather quickly, leaving twelve of the Cardinals on the list as unassigned, a new category Lee had marked *UA*. As they went back through this list again, it became apparent that they did indeed need the help of the four men originally considered as possible additions to their group. They felt a little like the disciples when they had gathered to select the right man to replace Judas. Now they had an additional task of deciding who would contact each of these four men and how they would bring them up to speed on the task.

"How much do we tell them?" was Connors' question "Do we let them know about Ferranti's plot to overthrow the Pope, or do we just discuss the issue of the Pope's proposals?"

It was agreed that they needed to bring all four men together and tell them the whole story. If they were to be 'disciples,' they needed to know everything! But, it would have to be done quickly. Castle felt certain that all of the men would agree to have lunch together, and he wanted to host them in his rooms tomorrow.

"Is that wise?" Mulholland queried. "I am not certain your rooms are safe."

"You are right, my friend. We need a neutral spot."

Lee immediately offered his rooms. While the guest suites were not as luxurious as those of Castle and Mulholland, permanently assigned to the Vatican as Bishop Cardinals, Lee's suite was perfect. It would not be bugged, would not attract attention since Lee was a new and fairly unknown Cardinal, and it was in a rather remote wing so the men would probably not be noticed coming and going. Assignments were quickly made; Castle would call Perez and Bastiani, Connors would call his friend Van Leuk and Romano would contact Wallace, who had been made a Cardinal at the same time Romano was elevated. Lee would order a light lunch to be served at 11:30 and they would end with tea at 3 p.m., giving the men time to start their calls by late afternoon. This added step would take more time away from the calls the other eight had to complete, but they each planned to start early the next morning and to schedule the most crucial of their meetings for later tomorrow afternoon and well into the night. There would be little sleep for the eight over the next few days, but after tomorrow's lunch, there would be four more sleepless but empowered men in the Vatican.

Before adjourning for the evening, Lee and Castle agreed to prepare the materials that would be needed for tomorrow's lunch meeting and the two went off to Castle's suite to begin printing documents from Castle's laptop computer. He had not wanted any of these materials to be found anywhere on the Vatican servers, so everything had been done on his laptop, which he locked in his bedroom safe whenever he was not using it.

The next morning, after his usual oatmeal breakfast, George began his calls; he had arranged to meet with three men between the time that their lunch and tea would end around 4 p.m. and a late dinner with Cardinal Johansson of Sweden. He had left messages for those who were traveling today with suggested times for meetings the following day, allowing for a late start, knowing that most of them men would be suffering from jet lag, and giving himself time to check in with the others over breakfast. John XXIV was due to arrive that evening, returning from a retreat he had arranged in Tuscany so he would be refreshed and prayerful before the Council started. He had asked George to join him for prayer and dialogue in his suite at 10:30 p.m.. After checking his email, around ten in the morning, George retired to his bedroom to take a brief nap before lunch, knowing it would be a long day ahead.

As Castle walked down the long hall to Lee's rooms, he met Connors and Van Leuk walking just ahead of him. The three men entered Lee's suite together, followed shortly thereafter by Wallace. Bastiani and Perez were already there, chatting with Fernandez in rapid Spanish. Romano had also arrived early and was standing by the window with Lee. Brahatta and Mannion arrived about five minutes later and Mulholland, uncharacteristically, arrived last. Castle was certain that Mulholland was making calls up to the last minute, thereby explaining his tardiness. Of course, he wasn't really late; it was just a few minutes after 11:30 when Mulholland completed the scene. Castle allowed himself a moment of whimsy as he pictured John XXIV walking in on this scene and positioning the thirteen men in a 'Last

Supper' pose. But he knew that John was still in Tuscany, and that had he known of this meeting, he would have made sure he was not present. This Pope preferred to eschew the typical Vatican politics and put everything in the hands of the Holy Spirit. Although Castle did not consider for a moment that he was a political animal and certainly felt the Spirit guided the Church on a daily basis, he had been at the Vatican long enough to know that nothing got done without the machinations of the political hierarchy.

As the men sat down to lunch, there was an air of excitement in the room. Lee again took over with an explanation of why the men had been called together, outlined the timeframe for the meeting and then introduced Castle, who would take over from there. As Castle welcomed the men and thanked them for their service, Lee handed out the folders containing the same information that the eight had received what seemed like an eternity ago, but was a matter of mere days. Castle, with the assistance of Mulholland, outlined what they had learned about Ferranti's plan to not only defeat John's proposals, but to overthrow the Pope himself! The men were all shocked, and Perez was extremely agitated at the very thought of this plot. Perez was an emotional man under normal circumstances, one with a great devotion to his faith and to the Papacy, and this revelation actually brought him to tears.

"How can this be? How could anyone presume to attempt such an outrage?"

He lapsed into Spanish as he began praying and holding his ears so as not to hear any more of this obscenity.

Castle thought of the prophets who rent their garments and plucked their beards when hearing of humankind's unfaithfulness to God. The men were all moved by Perez's display of emotion and Castle praised God for Perez's devotion, which inspired all of them, especially the eight who were physically and emotionally exhausted right now. Perez took his seat, apologetic for his emotional outburst. Castle assured him that they all felt the same and that he was personally grateful to Perez for clarifying their feelings and inspiring them to go on with the task ahead of them. Lee was then given the task of reporting on their activities over the past few days, and now the rather frantic calls received by each of the four men began to make sense.

After lunch, they adjourned to the small sitting room where they first prayed about the task ahead of them. It was, Castle thought, beginning to feel more and more like the Last Supper. Although the key figure was not here in the flesh, they could feel the Spirit in the room. Perhaps it was more of a Pentecostal experience, thought Castle. After a long and emotional prayer, in which each of the men participated either aloud or in his heart, Lee pulled the well-guarded list out of his folder, and Castle asked him to go through it with the full cohort. Each of the new men enthusiastically accepted assignments, eager to do their part, perhaps a bit regretful that they were not in on the initial meetings. None of them felt ignored, however. They understood that this work couldn't have waited for them to arrive physically in the Vatican and that it certainly was not a discussion to have by phone.

By the time they had gone through the list, talked about the meetings some of them had already held that morning, and where each of the original eight was on their assigned calls, it was time for tea. Lee had ordered a large urn of green tea and an assortment of Chinese almond cookies and Italian biscotti and pizzelles, along with some hazelnut cookies rolled in confectioner's sugar, a Mexican treat. A plate of fresh fruit completed the service. Castle helped Lee pour tea and again thanked the men for their willingness to be a part of this important task. There was some discussion revolving around the Ferranti document they had obtained from an undisclosed source, and how they could address this plot in the Council. They knew this would require a more lengthy discussion and there was no time for that now. They had a lot of work to do! Lee suggested that they establish their next meeting time and that the agenda for that meeting would include a short report on their calls, but the bulk of the meeting would be devoted to developing a strategy for the Council itself. All agreed that this made the most sense, and they established a meeting for the night before the Council, an early dinner in Van Leuk's suite. Like Lee's, his suite was in a remote section of the Vatican and one that would not be noticed or subject to a lot of traffic.

Bastiani asked if he might close the meeting with a prayer and led the group in a deeply spiritual, scripture-based prayer asking for the guidance that the Holy Sprit had given the early apostles, and calling on the early Popes who suffered much for their beliefs. They departed in silence, as each was wrapped in his own thoughts and still in awe of the depth of Bastiani's prayer.

Chapter 19

Reno, Nevada

Leslie had made all the arrangements for her trip to Rome; she needed to meet with George before he came to Connecticut in September for the big event at Foxwoods. But there was one thing she had to do before she met with George. She left the travel agent's office and headed south on Route 395. Her overnight bag was in the car and she had her plug-in cooler stocked with enough water and food for three days. She had to head back to the Matriarch; she needed to know if she was on the right track. She felt she had the first two questions answered for her. Runningwater and Barton had set the wheels in motion for two of the biggest projects imaginable, bigger than anything that had been undertaken by anyone in their respective fields, bigger than Leslie, bigger than all of them. In just a few months, the event Runningwater was staging would serve as the impetus to bring every Native American casino in the country, along with others in the gaming industry, together to fund environmental projects so sweeping they could reverse all the damage humankind had done to God's creation over the past thousands of years. And, soon after, in Laramie, Barton and members of the technology and entertainment industries would establish a funding stream to fight hatred and bigotry by reaching young people to recognize and celebrate diversity. She had been given the ideas and the means to implement these ideas and now one thing remained for Leslie—to figure out what the third mandate from God had been, "Return My Church to the Prophets and Mystics." She thought at times that maybe she had it wrong, maybe she had misunderstood, although deep in her heart, she knew that those were the exact words; she just didn't know how to deal with them.

As she drove those familiar roads, her earlier trip came rushing back into her mind, consuming her thoughts. She had decided she would stop by that wonderful lake again and see if it still had that same magical quality of throwing off a perfect reflection of its surroundings. Since her last trip, she had been reading a lot about St. Catherine of

Siena and she recalled Catherine's words about gazing into the water until you became the water. Leslie wondered if the lake was a metaphor for her life. Perhaps we are all called to be a perfect reflection of the world around us, she thought, as she climbed the steep hill to where she knew the lake would be waiting. She had again brought a crisp salad, some tuna and an apple; she had timed the trip so she could have lunch by the lake. This time, however, she would stay the night in Bishop and then get a very early start so she might even visit Methuselah before her pilgrimage to the Matriarch. She thought of the photograph of Methuselah in Joseph Runningwater's office. After the event in September, she had planned to stay in Connecticut for a visit with family and friends and Joseph had already decided that the two of them would spend a day together to debrief and plan their next steps. This would give her an opportunity to ask him about the photograph, although, she knew that if she introduced the subject, he would ask to hear her story, and she wasn't at all sure she could tell him yet. Anyway, she wouldn't have too much time to spend back East, because there was the Laramie project coming up and she wondered if after today and her trip to Rome, she might have an altogether different path to follow. She just knew that she would follow on whatever path the Matriarch led her.

The lake was exactly as she had remembered it. Leslie jumped out of her X Terra, grabbed her picnic blanket and basket. This time, she had even brought a small bottle of wine to sip while she enjoyed her cheese and apple. And she had a wine glass, a container of cinnamon to sprinkle on the apple, and a special treat—the book of Catherine of Siena's prayers to read while she ate her dessert. The sun was warm and comforting as she ate lunch and for minute, she wished she could just lie down by the lake and take a nap, but she had to keep moving. Besides, a woman asleep on the ground in such a remote place might not be safe from wild animals or any stray humans who happened to be wandering by. Leslie did close her eyes for a few minutes before she popped the cork on the wine, cut her apple and cheese, and opened her book. She checked her watch before she started reading, knowing she could easily get lost in Catherine's prayers. She had vowed to only spend forty minutes here by the lake, no more, or she would be late getting into Bishop.

As she walked towards her car, she felt as though she were leaving a dear friend. The lake had become an important part of this trip, like that of a loving aunt who helped one find their way to peace though connecting with one's family. She looked fondly over her shoulder and even raised her hand to wave a loving goodbye to the lake. Had anyone been watching her, they would have taken her for being a bit odd, if not downright crazy. But the gesture came naturally, and besides, the road was deserted. Leslie was starting to think that nature was becoming more important to her than people, and she wanted to make sure that her relationship with the lake, the mountains and the trees did not take precedence over her family and friends, and anyone who needed her.

She checked into the motel in Bishop a few hours later, the same one she had stayed at last trip, and decided she would linger over a nice dinner at the rustic bar and grill next to the motel, remembering the great meal she had had there the last time. She had found that these places often had better meals and much better prices than some of the fine dining establishments she visited. The bar was filled mostly with truck drivers passing through and likely staying at the same motel, and a few locals, mostly men, with a smattering of women that her mother would have called, 'barflies.' A few of the truck drivers were at the bar, but most were seated at tables enjoying a hot meal, including a husband and wife couple seated at the table next to Leslie's. They were in their sixties, thought Leslie, and she looked at them with envy. She remembered that she and Michael had often talked about what a great life it would be for a husband and wife whose children were grown to travel the highways together on long haul trips, seeing the country while they worked, taking turns driving. They were both dressed in jeans and fleece vests and both wore cowboy boots. They seemed very much in love, and again, Leslie felt envious; she missed Michael so much.

The woman smiled when Leslie sat down and after the waitress had taken Leslie's order, the woman looked her way and asked,

"Traveling through here on business?"

Leslie smiled back, "Well sort of; I write for travel magazines and visited here a few months ago to do a story on the Ancient Bristlecone Forest. I didn't finish and decided to come back again to get more information."

Not really an untruth, but not quite the whole story.

"Where are you from?" Leslie inquired.

"Iowa. We're driving that big rig parked between the motel and here, the purple one—my wife's choice. I'm Frank and this is Dorothy. Pleased to meet you, Ma'am."

Frank was a burly guy with a soft southern drawl that Leslie suspected did not originate in Iowa.

"Where are you from originally?" she asked.

"Alabama. I guess you can tell that!"

Dorothy added, "I met Frank when he was stationed at Leavenworth, and I lived near there at the time."

"Yeah, I am sure glad to be away from the prison system. I had been a guard for thirteen years, when we decided to buy our first rig and see the country. So we bought a home in Iowa, close to Dolly's family, but we don't spend much time there."

Leslie could see he was much happier with this arrangement than he ever was guarding prisoners.

"You know, my husband and I often talked about what great fun it would be to do what you and Dolly are doing. We enjoyed many great driving trips together when Michael was alive. In fact, it was one of our trips out west that prompted me to move to Nevada after he died. We were originally from New England."

"I'm sorry to hear about your husband. Did he die recently?" Dorothy sympathized.

"Seven years ago, but sometimes it seems like yesterday."

Leslie grew sad for a minute, but then, as her food arrived, she perked up and started a cheerier conversation.

"So tell me, what have you seen on this trip?"

"You mean, besides motel rooms, restaurants, and truck stop rest rooms?" Dorothy laughed. "Well, we haven't seen the bristlecones, but we've seen the Grand Canyon, Yosemite, Yellowstone, the Joshua Trees, and Death Valley. We have a delivery to make in San Andreas and one in Sacramento. Then we'll be heading back home, but maybe we'll visit those trees before we head on home."

By the time they had finished dinner and each decided they needed to get to bed for their early starts the next day, Leslie concluded that she hadn't enjoyed a conversation more in a long time, and as she said goodnight to Frank and Dolly, she wished she could just throw her bag in the back of their big rig and travel with them for a while. But she knew her destiny was waiting for her in the Bristlecone Forest. She closed the door to her room, put on her pajamas and settled under the covers to read for a while, but she drifted off to sleep around nine o'clock.

The next morning was a repeat of that first trip except that she had a much earlier start this time; she wanted every minute in the forest that she could squeeze into the extended hours of daylight this trip afforded. She arrived at the top of the hill where the visitor's center stood, and decided that she would hike to see Methuselah this time before making her pilgrimage to the Matriarch. She had to be able to tell Runningwater that she had seen the oldest of the trees on this trip. She thought of that visit in his office and before she started her hike, she pulled the well-worn poem from her wallet and read it again. She wondered about John Lame Deer. Could he somehow be connected to Runningwater, to her? Certainly the three were connected in spirit, if not by blood. With Lame Deer's words in her head, she hiked past hundreds of bristlecones until she reached the spot where Methuselah stood. He was indeed impressive, and while she revered him for his age and enduring spirit, she had no compulsion to embrace him as she had the Matriarch. In fact, she took about a dozen photos of Methuselah; something she felt would have been obscene with the Matriarch. She knew that the sun was getting higher and she wanted to be at the grove where the Matriarch stood by high noon. She wasn't sure why, but she somehow felt that she needed the brightest, hottest sun on her back when she made her return to the Great Mother. She headed down the trail loop toward the visitors center. It would take her more than an hour, even though she walked fast. Along the way, she felt the presence of her ancestors, Greta, Petra, Anna, and all the rest, especially Katrina and Woqobi Muguwa. She also felt a new presence walking with her, Catherine of Siena. The meaning of this new spiritual guide was unclear to her, but she knew there was a meaning.

When she returned to the visitor's center, she was amazed that the park ranger remembered her from her earlier trip.

"You got to see Methuselah this time?"

Joan Grabitz prided herself on her photographic memory, but even she usually didn't remember every visitor to the Bristlecone Forest. But she had remembered Leslie very clearly. She recalled Leslie's disappointment when she realized she would not be able to hike to see Methuselah before the sun set. She had suggested to Leslie that she drive to the grove where the Matriarch stood instead. Most people were not particularly interested in making that trek over the winding dirt road, and the grove was usually deserted, but that is what made it so attractive. Joan knew that the Matriarch called those whom she wanted to come to her and she felt the Matriarch was calling Leslie, so that day she had hoped Leslie would make the trip. She knew now that Leslie had indeed made the trip, otherwise, why had she returned so soon? Joan very seldom saw visitors more than once unless they were scientists.

"Yes," replied Leslie, "I did get to see Methuselah. I have a friend who recommended I come back and allow time for the hike. But I am heading back up to the Matriarch's grove now."

"Of course you are; I knew you would be back."

Leslie was dumbfounded. How could this park ranger remember her, with the thousands of people who must have crossed her path over the past months? And how did she know Leslie would be back? She must have sensed in Leslie something of the experience she had had that day. Leslie was afraid to speak, lest she blurt out the whole story to this stranger, but she felt that Joan already knew it. Although neither of them had told each other their names, she knew the rangers name was Joan even before she glanced at the name badge on Joan's chest pocket. Perhaps Joan had visited the Matriarch and had had a similar experience. Suddenly Leslie envied this woman who lived in the shadow of these elders and could visit the Matriarch whenever she wanted.

"I guess I'd better get moving. I want to get there by noon," Leslie said, looking at her watch.

Although the two women had spoken just a few sentences to each other and had only seen each other twice, for some reason they embraced before Leslie walked out the door. When Leslie glanced back, Joan had a serene smile on her face and Leslie could sense her pleasure and excitement. She turned around and ran back to the visitor's center and handed Joan her business card. She hadn't thought she really needed business cards to be a freelance writer, but Valerie had convinced her she needed business cards and a website in order to be taken seriously. Valerie had set up the website for her, but Leslie had always thought it was too much trouble to keep it up to date, so it was sadly out of date. But she usually did remember to put business cards in her wallet and carry a few extras in her car.

The drive to the grove where the Matriarch stood was much like her last trip, except that this time, she did not feel the hurriedness. She knew what awaited her and she knew there was no rush to get there— the Matriarch would be waiting. Again, she heard the music in her head and even smelled incense. Although she drove more slowly than she had the last time, it seemed she reached the grove in less time than her last trip had taken.

The Matriarch was bathed in the noonday sun. There was one other car there this time and its occupants, two young men and two young women were walking around the grove and the dark haired woman was taking lots of photos with expensive, professional-looking camera equipment. One of the men had just coming out of the rustic rest room and looked eager to get moving. He spoke to the blond woman and she walked over to the dark haired woman and they started gathering up the camera equipment and walking towards the car. Leslie was relieved. She was afraid the Matriarch would feel violated and might not be willing to communicate with her as she had on that fateful day that seemed an eternity ago.

As the four climbed in their car, they nodded and smiled at Leslie and Leslie smiled back, but she hoped they did not start a conversation. As they drove down the hill, a bit too fast, they stirred up a lot of dust and Leslie was glad they were gone. She was sure they meant no harm, but she felt cheated that they had robbed her of the first sight of the Matriarch standing alone in the noonday sun.

Again, Leslie sat on the edge of the front seat and removed her boots and socks. This time, she circled the tree, walking in an inward spiral, much like a walk through a labyrinth. The closer she got, the clearer her thoughts became. She was beginning to understand the meaning of the last of the three mandates she had been given, "Return My Church to the Prophets and Mystics." She had a sudden revelation that was so basic and yet had evaded her thoughts until now. Jesus, she now understood, was the primordial Prophet and Mystic of the Church and that the call to her Church was to return to the Church of Jesus, to become what the early Church had been, before all the hierarchy and the all consuming love for power had corrupted so many within the Church. At first she wasn't certain how this would be accomplished and she certainly could not envision how she could bring it about. But the closer she got to the Matriarch, the more she absorbed of God's plan.

It was amazingly simple, much like that of the first two plans that had already been put into motion. As she got within inches of the Matriarch, the heat came at her like sparks of a campfire, and she feared for a minute that she might be incinerated. Then, a cooling breeze swept over her, enveloping her body and her spirit. She floated towards the Matriarch and embraced her, kissing her smooth bark and running her hands up and down the great tree's trunk, stroking her, as one would stroke a lover. This time, she would not be called to enter the tree; there was no need now. She had already entered into the Great Mystery. Now what was left for her to do was to share that mystery with George and with the Church.

Chapter 20

Vatican City

Leslie was eager to see George and perhaps even more eager to share all that was happening in her own life. And yet, she knew there was already a lot happening in the Church and wanted to hear George's story even before she shared her own. She dressed carefully, in casual but stylish attire, a short, yet modest, black light wool skirt, black tights and black leather shoes with low, square heels, topped with the white cashmere turtleneck sweater she had worn in Laramie. She wore her grandmother's gold bracelet and a small locket on a long chain that had been Greta's. The locket had photos of her parents and was Leslie's favorite piece of jewelry.

George had sent a driver for her again and as she entered George's suite, she drew a few furtive glances from some of the Vatican staff that were unaccustomed to a woman alone entering the suite of a Cardinal. George was standing by the window when she entered the room, and immediately ran towards her to embrace her. They hugged for several minutes, neither of them wanting to let go of the other. Leslie couldn't remember the last time they had been alone together and it felt good to be here with George. He had always been her rock, especially after Michael died. She couldn't wait to pour out her story and George couldn't wait to hear it. But first he wanted to bring Leslie up to speed on what was happening in the Church. They sat by the fireplace with a glass of wine before dinner and George excitedly told her about the happenings at the Vatican in recent months.

The Council had ended just two weeks ago and it had been an amazing event. Leslie, like most of the world, was aware of the Pope's commitment to eliminating the AIDS pandemic and she knew that this Council was called to address that issue. The press had gone crazy with the rumors about the Pope's proposal to allow priests to marry and his further proposal to consider ordaining women. Although no one thought this last concept had a serious chance of being adopted by this group of Cardinals, it was a milestone that it would even come before a Council. Leslie didn't know much more than what she had read in the newspapers and heard on television. She had gotten a little of the background from George in their phone conversation, but his email had been nonexistent during the Council, and she knew that he would be working into the wee hours of the morning on Church business, so they were both glad they had this time to catch up.

He filled her in on the proceedings of the Council, glossing over the workings of The Twelve, as they had referred to themselves. The Pope's AIDS plan had been adopted with an overwhelming majority of the Cardinals throwing their support behind it. This would cost the Church more money than it had ever spent on anything since the Crusades, if you compared their cost in today's dollars. Like the Crusades, which were supported by many for political reasons, this plan was already gathering support from many of the world's wealthier governments.

Most of the world had been stunned by the removal of the celibacy requirement for priests. Leslie had known from George before the rest of the world, that this was in the works, but she doubted it would actually happen. After her last trip to the Matriarch, which coincidentally was happening at almost the very minute that the Council voted on the celibacy issue, Leslie understood that the Church had to be restored to be the Church God intended it to be. George shared some of the work he had been doing over the past months.

"We had the best minds in the Church working on this for many years, researching how the Church came to abandon its early roots when both men and women, both married and single persons, served as disciples. Of course, our 'opposition,' headed by Cardinal Ferranti, did their own research as well and had their case for retaining a male, celibate priesthood as well prepared as ours."

Leslie knew that Ferranti had been a thorn in George's side since he had arrived at the Vatican and that he had fought every reform of this Pope and Cardinal Castle, tooth and nail. She worried about George getting caught up in Vatican politics, which she knew could be dangerous, but George had always laughed and told her she read too many mystery books. But she sensed that perhaps for the first time, George had taken the dangers of Vatican politics seriously. She could tell that he was purposely not giving her the full story, not because of limited time or his eagerness to hear her story, but more because he didn't want to cause her concern.

"Well, yours was guided by the Holy Spirit, and that made all the difference."

She knew, however, that there was perhaps an equal mix of divine guidance and human politics that went into this victory. And indeed it was a victory, not for George or even for the Pope, but for the Church, and for all humankind.

"So, what's next, now that the Council is over?"

Leslie wondered if George would have more free time or less now that this huge step had been taken.

"Well, I would like to say that I'm relieved that it is all over, but of course, it is just beginning. I will be coming to the States for a while to meet with the National Conference of Bishops and then I am off to Canada and New Zealand, where we think they will be ready to implement the changes before the rest of the world. You know how eager the Americans are to get things rolling. Some of the Europeans will be ready soon, too, but the Latin Americans and the Asians will take a little longer. Many of the Latin Americans are pretty traditional as a whole and the Asians don't accept change lightly, but the support is there. They are in favor of the changes; they just need to talk things through. And the Africans have so many other issues to worry about that they may not have the resources to implement it right away, but they are so relieved that the AIDS Plan was implemented, and so grateful to John for his understanding of their needs, that they will implement the changes with little resources and even less discussion."

"So you will be a real globe trotter for the next few years."

Leslie wished he could be with her during the next several years and not off meeting with Bishops and Cardinals. But she knew this was George's destiny as well as she knew her own.

"Of course, you know I am dying to find out what happened on the ordination of women."

George knew this would be a key issue for Leslie and he had deliberately saved it for last.

"As you've heard through the news media, the question was hotly debated and although it wasn't ratified, it was not rejected either. Basically, what you've heard and read pretty much sums it up. It will be discussed in the second session of the Council, next year. I must say it was more positive than we had hoped. John, of course, is ecstatic and has pretty much secluded himself in prayer since the Council. I am certain what he is praying for is a speedy approval at the next session of the Council. We were all stunned that the Cardinals agreed to a second session of the Council so quickly on the heels of this one. You have no idea how much these gatherings take out of all of us, but especially the Pope. He does, however want to meet with you while you're here and we are having lunch with him tomorrow."

Leslie had no idea how much of her conversation with George he had shared with the Pope, but she was delighted that apparently he had shared enough to pique John's interest. Of course she had not shared the entire story with George and she knew she had to give him the whole picture before their lunch with the Pope. She had told George of her first trip to the Matriarch and how she suddenly had this 'gift' or perhaps it was a curse, of hearing people's thoughts. She had not told him about the butterflies and the birds or of her ride with Mancha. She now told him all the details, and filled him in on the details of the two projects she had coming up. Although George had heard some of this before, he was amazed at the depth of Leslie's commitment and the intricacies of her plans. After hearing her story, George agreed that she had had some sort of vision and that this new ability of hers was definitely a gift from God. He sensed, however, that there was much more to hear from Leslie. But then he suddenly found himself very tired.

"Look at the time; I can't believe it's after midnight."

George really didn't want to end this conversation, and he knew Leslie well enough to know that she had more to tell and that she would have saved the 'best' for last. That was her style.

"I know. I should be tired, but I think I could stay up all night, there is so much more to tell."

She really wanted to continue tonight but she could see the lines around George's eyes and mouth were growing deeper and she knew that the past few months had been very hard on him, despite the positive outcome. He had never liked confrontation and this business with Ferranti must have just about killed him.

"But I guess we really should get some rest," She said almost sadly.

Of course, she doubted she would get much rest tonight, but she knew George was ready to call it a night. They said goodnight and he walked Leslie to the reception lobby where her driver was waiting.

On the drive back to her hotel, she asked the driver to take the long way, so she could see Rome at night. The Coliseum was lit up and there were still tourists wandering around. Leslie asked the driver if he would wait while she walked around a bit. Although, he looked at her rather strangely, he of course agreed; this was, after all, Cardinal Castle's sister.

"Of course, Signora," He reluctantly agreed.

He dropped her off and agreed to wait, knowing he would not let her out of his sight. It really wasn't safe for a woman to be alone at this hour on the streets of Rome; in fact, it was hardly safe in broad daylight for her to be wandering the ruins alone. But Leslie didn't seem a bit afraid. She bounced out of the car and walked slowly towards the Coliseum. It looked eerily like it was alive with the people who had filled it seats thousands of years before; she could almost hear the shouting. The three-quarter moon lighted the steps well enough for her to climb without fear. Her driver, Sergio Santini, watched with trepidation as she climbed. How would he explain to the Cardinal if anything happened to his sister. But he need not have feared. Leslie was gone just about ten minutes when she returned to the car and Santini, grateful to have her safely in his back seat, closed the door and almost ran around the car to the driver's door. He was happy to leave this part of town and deliver Leslie safely to her hotel. He walked her to the door and handed her over to the doorman, whose somber face betrayed no questioning, no judgment on his part as to why the Cardinal's sister was arriving home alone at 1:30 in the morning. Leslie closed the door to her room, called downstairs for a 6 a.m. wake-up call, and quickly stripped off her clothes, slipped on her pajamas, and jumped under the covers. The brief walk at the Coliseum had been just the right amount of brisk fresh air she needed to help her sleep.

She was up and about fifteen minutes before the wake-up call. In fact, she had brushed her teeth, gotten her clothes ready and had a cup of tea before the phone rang. As soon as she answered the wake-up call, she jumped into the shower and let the hot water wash away the sleepiness and the tiredness. She dried herself with the thick terry cloth towel and dressed quickly, as usual, feeling totally refreshed. She headed downstairs and decided to enjoy a hearty breakfast in the hotel. Santini was not scheduled to pick her up until 8:30, so she even had time to read several sections of the book she had brought along, *Catherine of Siena: The Dialogue*, during breakfast.

By the time Santini arrived, Leslie was already getting anxious to meet with George. As expected, her driver was right on time and he was happy to see her. She knew she had caused him a bit of anxiety last evening when she insisted on walking alone at the Coliseum, but he showed no anger or uneasiness this morning. Leslie climbed into the back seat of the black Mercedes and opened the glass partition between her and Santini.

"How long have you been working at the Vatican?" she inquired, with sincerity in her voice.

Santini, delighted by her genuine interest in him, responded.

"Actually, Signora, I have been here since I was eighteen years old. I started by washing cars. My older brother was a priest and he got me a job here to try to keep me out of trouble. I guess I was a bit of a rowdy youth and he was worried that I would bring shame on my family if he didn't get me away from the streets. We both knew I wasn't cut out for the priesthood, but I loved working here and it wasn't long before I started running errands in the Vatican cars. I am now the senior driver for the Cardinals, second only to the driver of the Pope's own car."

The pride in his voice was apparent to Leslie.

In a talkative mood, he went on.

"I understand you have a son who is studying for the priesthood. Cardinal Castle must have had a great influence on him."

Leslie was always happy to talk about her children, and wanted to assure Santini that she was equally as proud of all her children.

"Yes, my youngest has one more year in the seminary before he becomes a priest. My older son is a successful businessman and my daughter is an engineer. Cardinal Castle has actually had an impact on all of us. He is a very special man."

"You don't need to tell me that. It is my honor to serve as his personal driver. I have been here for the reigns of three Popes and have driven many Cardinals during that time, but the current Holy Father and Cardinal Castle are by far the two who have influenced me, as well as the Church, in a most positive way. Although I worked in the Vatican, I never went to church much because I felt the Church was not relevant in my life. Since this Pope has been in office, and after serving your brother, I have been renewed in my faith."

"That is good to hear. I'll bet you could tell a lot of stories about the men you've driven over the years," Leslie suggested with a smile.

"I sure could, but, as you Americans say, 'If I told you, I'd have to kill you.'"

They both laughed at that, but Leslie suspected there might be a hint of truth in his comment. Before she could inquire any further of Santini, he had pulled into a reserved parking space and quickly came around to open the door for Leslie. George was waiting for her and she could see he hadn't slept much last night.

George thought Leslie looked as though she had slept for twelve hours, although of course he knew all about her early morning visit to the Coliseum.

"Sleep well," he asked?

"Yes, like a baby." Of course he had never been up all night with an infant to know how silly this analogy was.

"Well, I didn't get much sleep," he added, knowing that his tiredness showed on his face. "I couldn't wait to hear 'the rest of the story.' And since we don't have much time before we meet with John, let's get right to it."

Leslie hardly knew where to start, but she was aware that George wanted and needed to hear this before they talked with the Pope. So she launched right in with the story of her latest trip to the bristlecones.

"You know I had three mandates from the Matriarch, from God. And, that the third one had me mystified from the very beginning. It seemed like the first two just fell into place, almost without me doing anything. And these two projects are well on their way to fulfillment. But I spent a lot of sleepless nights myself thinking about what that third part could mean, and how could I possibly do anything about returning the Church to what Yahweh meant it to be? So I knew I needed to make another trip to the Matriarch.

This time I went first to see Methuselah, the oldest living thing on earth. I somehow thought that maybe because that tree was older, it, too, would have a special message for me that might clarify things. Impressive as Methuselah is, he didn't speak to me. So I headed back to the Matriarch."

Leslie then told George of the message she got on that second visit. Different as it was from the first visit, it was equally revelatory. When she had finished her story, George no longer looked tired. In fact, his face had a glow that Leslie likened to the Transfiguration. She was afraid she would have to cover his face with a veil before they left his quarters lest people would stare at them. She knew that glow; she had felt it after her two visits to the Matriarch. They needed to leave now for their meeting with John. As they walked the short distance to the Pope's private quarters, a place where Leslie suspected not too many women had visited, they were both unusually quiet.

John greeted them at the door himself; he was alone in his rooms, having sent his assistant on an errand he knew would take all afternoon. He was delighted to see Leslie again. The last time they were all together was when George had received his Papal appointment, which was celebrated with a special Mass. John remembered how impressed he was at the time with Cardinal Castle's sister. She was a delightful woman, and one whose faith was apparent. Her three children, including Andre, who was studying for the priesthood, had accompanied her on that trip. And John had found the entire family impressive.

"Signora Flynn, it is so good to see you again."

He greeted her with a kiss on each cheek. And then he clutched her two hands in his for a full minute.

"Cardinal Castle tells me you've had an 'experience,' shall we say? I find the word, 'vision' so overused. I am eager to hear all about it."

They talked about the Council and the AIDS plan during lunch. Leslie also filled John in on her own two big plans about which he had heard some of the details from George. She didn't realize how much time they had spent on lunch until she glanced at the clock and found it had been almost two-and-a-half hours since they had entered the room. They were enjoying coffee and tea looking out over the piazza when John leaned close and his voice was almost a whisper.

"Tell me, Leslie, what are we to do about this 'mandate' as you call it?"

Leslie was stunned. George had told him more than she realized. When, she was not certain, but they must have had a conversation while she had stepped out for a brief visit to the ladies' room. But of course, he couldn't have told the Pope the whole story in so short a time. How did the Pope know of this? Was he perhaps privy to her and George's private discussion or had he had a similar 'experience' himself?

He saw that Leslie was taken aback and quickly went on.

"George has told me about the message from the Matriarch, and I am intrigued. I believe you have truly received a message from God and I also believe that we must do something about it. Tell me more about this wonderful thing that is happening to you, to the Church, to all of us."

They spent the rest of the afternoon and into the evening talking, praying, laughing, crying, the three of them together. The sun had set and John suddenly realized how long they had been together.

"Forgive me, Leslie, I should have ordered dinner in for us, but not to worry. I will order something now, and we can continue our discussions. You probably both need a break. As you know, the rest rooms are over there," he said, pointing behind him, "and please help yourself to a drink from the bar. George, you know where everything is." He went to the phone and spoke in rapid Italian, then excused himself and headed in the direction of his bedroom.

Leslie and George fixed drinks, and were standing quietly by the window for a rather long time. Leslie was beginning to worry that the Pope was not coming back. Perhaps he had lain down for a nap, but then she noticed the light on the phone was lit, so she assumed that he had some business to attend to and he had gone into his bedroom to make phone calls.

"He likes you a lot, Leslie," George said, as handed her a drink. "He always has, and I know he will support you in this, whatever you decide to do."

Just then, there was a soft rap on the door, and George opened it to let in a young man pushing a table bearing their dinner. There were two bottles of wine, a white wine in a silver ice bucket and a red, wrapped in a white cloth, and numerous dishes covered with silver lids bearing the Papal coat of arms. It looked to Leslie like enough to feed about eight people. As the table was being prepared, John emerged from his room.

"So sorry to keep you waiting, but the Church never sleeps, or eats, it sometimes seems."

"No problem. We all needed a break." George smiled.

While they enjoyed dinner, Leslie told the Pope the remaining details of her 'experience' and what she felt the second trip to the Matriarch meant. They talked into the early morning hours about what all of this meant and how they would proceed. By the time she left John's room, Leslie was exhausted, but at the same time, invigorated by the future that lay ahead for all of them.

Chapter 21

Hartford, Connecticut

Sara was excited, but apprehensive, as she drove to Bradley airport to pick up Leslie. Although they had talked by phone and email, she hadn't seen her dear friend for several months and she knew by the sound of Leslie's voice when they did talk by phone that there was something different about her, something she couldn't quite put her finger on. The two had been friends for so long that they could just about read each other's thoughts; in fact, when they were young, they even had a special language that only the two of them understood, much like that of twins. But for some reason, now it seemed that although Leslie could still sense Sara's deepest feelings, there was an invisible barrier around Leslie that she could no longer read. Perhaps when they met face-to-face, either this nagging feeling that there was something wrong with Leslie would go away, or Sara would find that once again, they could share that special closeness they had always had. Sara had been busy working with Joseph Runningwater on the big event planned for a week from now, Labor Day weekend, and was thrilled to be a part of this project. Sara had always been interested in the environment and had spent time working as both a volunteer and a staff member of several environmental groups. It was, in fact, Sara who got Leslie interested in saving the earth and in organic foods and natural cures, although she knew that Leslie's maternal grandmother had also influenced her in that direction. Sara's enthusiasm and dedication to preserving the earth were the perfect compliment for Leslie's ability to create a vision and to plan out the details needed to make this vision a reality. The two of them, with Runningwater's power and wealth behind them, were about to pull off a phenomenal feat, one that could significantly change the world in which they lived. As she pulled into the short term parking area, she wondered if Leslie would look as different as she had sounded on the phone.

As Leslie headed towards the baggage claim area where Sara would be waiting, for just a fleeting moment she thought maybe she needed to sit down with Sara over tea and tell her the entire story. She banished that thought almost as soon as it entered her mind. First, there was no time to share her 'experience;' they had so much work to do before this weekend. And second, she still felt that she had to wait until she was back in Rome and George had confirmed all their plans before she talked to Sara or even her children about the future.

Andre had spent two weeks with Leslie before heading off for his summer assignment in New Mexico. She had shared her strange tale with Andre, except for the details of her last trip to the Bristlecone Forest, her trip to Rome and her conversation with George and Pope John XXIV. Even with Andre, she had been guarded about that part of her experience and about her plans for the future. It was too soon to tell him then. All of her children would be at the Foxwoods event next weekend and she planned to have a family dinner with them on Tuesday to let them know what was happening. She also planned to talk with Joseph Runningwater and Fred Simms later that week, when they had their 'post mortem' event meeting. And of course, she would meet with Sara the day after the family dinner. All the pieces were in place, but the focus right now had to be on a successful event. And she also wanted to recruit Sara to help with the Laramie event as soon as the Foxwoods event was out of the way.

As soon as Sara saw Leslie coming towards her, she knew there was something very different about her. It was even more apparent in person than it had been on the phone. Sara was convinced that Leslie was in love. She hadn't seen her look this happy since Michael died. In fact, she didn't know if she had ever seen Leslie this happy, even when she and Michael had first met. It had to be Joseph Runningwater; Leslie was always talking about how wonderful he was. So that was it! Well, it was about time Leslie thought of starting a serious relationship; she had hardly even dated since Michael died. Sara couldn't wait to se the two of them together.

"You look wonderful, Leslie. How do you do it?"

Sara, as slim and trim as Leslie, had always been the more attractive of the two of them, but time had been crueler to her than to Leslie. Leslie never seemed to wrinkle, and Sara envied her clear bright eyes and shiny, silky hair. Leslie told Sara is was because she took care of herself and ate right. Sara tried to eat healthy but she had lost interest in the organic food craze she had been so enthusiastic about in the sixties and seventies. And she never could give up cigarettes and caffeine. Two marriages and two divorces had also taken their toll on her. She had always envied Leslie and Michael's relationship. Why couldn't she find someone like Michael? Too bad he didn't have a brother. Sara's first husband, Barry, had been a womanizer, and after twelve years, she just couldn't put up with any more. After that divorce, she tried the single life for a while and then, after three years, gave love another try. Following a whirlwind courtship, which in hindsight was a big mistake, she had married John on a cruise ship off the coast of Barbados. Once they were home and John insisted that they invite his mother to come live with them, she knew she had a made a mistake but she stuck this one out for five years. Istead of working on their new married relationship, John went happily on with his relationship with 'Mother Tunney,' as John's mother insisted she be called. Feeling like an intruder in her own home, Sara quickly became convinced that married life just wasn't her destiny. She enjoyed her career and her volunteer activities and she dated often but never ventured into another serious relationship. She even had a fling with another woman, Terry, but decided that wasn't her cup of tea either. But throughout all of this, her relationship with Leslie never changed much, even though their lifestyles were very different. They could always count on each other and even though sometimes they didn't see each other for months, or even years, they always managed to pick up where they had left off and knew that no matter what, they would always be there for each other.

"Well, you're looking well yourself. How's your love life?"

It was Leslie's standard question to Sara every time they spoke.

They both laughed.

"Some things never change. Mine is just fine. Dating a great guy, Allen, but by the time this event is over, maybe I'll land a date with Joseph. He sure would be a catch for anyone."

She waited for Leslie's reaction; surely she would know if she had hit a sore spot with that comment. But Leslie didn't react the way she expected her to.

"That would be great, two of my favorite people, but somehow I don't think Joseph Runningwater has much time for dating." Leslie laughed.

Gathering her suitcase from the carousel, Leslie hooked her arm in Sara's, "Let's skip through the airport and see what all these staid business travelers think about that."

"Well, we always were good at creating a stir, weren't we?" Sara said, starting to feel like they were about forty years younger.

Somehow being with Leslie always made her feel like a teenager again.

"So tell me the answer to the big question, how is *your* love life? You must be dating someone by now."

"I have even less time to think about dating than Runningwater has. Besides this big event, I have another project that I want to talk to you about, but let's get this one off the ground first. And we are getting together Wednesday before the wrap up meeting at the casino on Thursday, right? I want us to compare notes before we meet with the others."

Leslie was being very evasive, and suddenly, instead of skipping arm in arm, they were two intense businesswomen entering into a very serious discussion. Leslie could be like that, Sara found, changing from a giddy girl one minute into a prim and proper woman the next. It was one of her more endearing qualities.

They hopped into Sara's little red Fiat sports car and headed to Valerie's where Leslie would be staying for a couple days before heading off to Mashantucket. She and Sara wanted to get everything done on their end before meeting with the casino event planners. There were a lot of phone calls to make and materials to put together. They planned to work for two solid days and then drive down to Foxwoods together. This would give them some time to catch up as well. And maybe, Leslie thought, she would break down and fill Sara in on the real scoop behind her recent activities. Although Leslie had promised herself she wanted to get this project completed before she even thought about the Laramie project, she was eager to get Sara involved in that, so she filled her in briefly on the ride to Valerie's, and she found Sara was eager to hear more. Sara was excited about this new venture, although it would take her out West, a place she could easily live without. She never understood Leslie's fascination with the wide-open spaces. They were a little too wide open for Sara; she never could understand why anyone, especially her friend Leslie, would want live on a ranch, miles from a mall, a spa or a Starbucks!

Valerie was happy to see Leslie and wanted to hear all about Rome and Uncle George, especially since she had been following the news about the Council. She put on the teapot and got out some fresh strawberries, goat cheese and crackers. Valerie had always loved Sara, and thought of her as an aunt, and she was happy to have her visit. Sara stopped in every once in a while to see the kids, whom she had sort of adopted as the grandchildren she would never have. Sara had an especially soft spot for Bunny and asked about her right away. She had brought Bunny a little ceramic Beatrix Potter rabbit, to add to her collection of rabbits. With little Michael down for his afternoon nap, the three women would have about an hour to relax before the older children came home.

Leslie filled them in on her trip to Rome and what she had learned from George about the Council, without mentioning her meetings with the Pope. Sara, she knew, would be kind of bored with all this discussion about Church politics so she tried to keep it light and short without disappointing Valerie, who had an intense interest in what was happening in Rome, partly because of her Uncle George, partly because of her brother Andre, and partly because she had fallen in love with Rome and all the trappings of the Vatican on her visit there several years ago. Sara was interested in her trip to the Coliseum, however, so Leslie spent some time telling them about her late night side trip. Sara, of course, wanted to know if she had done any shopping. Although she knew that Leslie hated to shop, she thought perhaps Rome might have tempted her to indulge in some of its famous shops.

By the time they had finished their tea and conversation, the girls had arrived home, first Bunny, from her day school, and then the older ones from 'real school' as Bunny called it. Leslie wasn't sure if Bunny was happier to see her or Sara, but the older children climbed onto Leslie's lap right away and started telling her about their day at school, while Sara and Bunny went to find a spot on Bunny's bookshelf for the latest rabbit in her collection. Valerie wanted Sara to stay for dinner, but she begged off, saying she had a lot of work to do before she and Leslie would meet in her home office tomorrow. And Leslie was just as happy to be able to have an early dinner and get to bed at a decent hour. She knew that if Sara stayed, they would talk well into the night.

The next two days, Leslie and Sara spent getting ready for the trip to Foxwoods. Sara tried several time to pry some news out of Leslie, baiting her again with the thought that she might be interested in Joseph Runningwater herself. But Leslie did not break down. She could be a real Sphinx when she wanted to be. Well, Sara was sure that when they arrived at Foxwoods and she saw them together, she would know for sure if there was anything going on between them. She had already noticed that Runningwater seemed to melt at the sound of Leslie's name, and that his face relaxed when he talked about her. She had also caught him glancing several times at the picture of the big tree on his wall when he talked about Leslie and there was a far off look in his eyes, as though he was sitting under that tree with Leslie.

The trip to Mashantucket was once again a delightful drive. Although it was late summer, there was already a brisk chill in the air and both Sara and Leslie had thrown cardigan sweaters over their short-sleeved shirts. They checked into the hotel and each of them rested in their own rooms for a while before dressing for dinner. Fred Simms, Jimmy Tall, Joseph Runningwater and Stephanie Trotter, the director of events, would be meeting them for dinner in Runningwater's suite in the hotel. Although he had a beautiful home in the country, he kept a suite at the hotel for late nights and business meetings. Leslie and Sara took the elevator up to the top floor, just one floor above their own adjoining rooms, and Leslie took deep breath as they knocked on the door to Runningwater's suite.

"Leslie, it has been too long," he greeted her with a long embrace. "And, Sara, my good friend and tireless worker," another embrace, although not as long or as intense as the one he gave Leslie.

They were the first to arrive, and Sara was unusually quiet as she studied the interaction between Runningwater and Leslie. She was certain of his attraction to Leslie, but Leslie was back in her Sphinx mode and she just couldn't read her friend's emotions at all. It was very disconcerting to Sara; she had always been able to know what her friend was thinking and feeling, and now she felt shut off from Leslie's world for some reason. Although Leslie was cordial and warm to Runningwater, she seemed to have a hesitancy that Sara couldn't understand, unless it was because of her. Perhaps Leslie did not want to reveal her feelings in front of Sara because she hadn't yet told Runningwater of her feelings for him. That had to be the answer, Sara was convinced. Just as this revelation came upon Sara, there was another tap on the door, and Fred Simms arrived. Fred was glad to see Leslie, and Sara immediately sensed that he, too, was attracted to Leslie, although she had not picked up any of this as she worked with Fred over these past months. Sara was a bit mystified, recalling that when they were growing up, it was always Sara who had this effect on men, and now, suddenly, she felt like the ugly stepsister while Leslie seemed to have turned into Cinderella. Not that she resented Leslie at all; she just couldn't figure out why all of a sudden all these men seemed so attracted to her. Well, if Jimmy Tall showed this same magnetic attraction, she would really start to worry.

Jimmy's arrival a few minutes later put Sara at ease. Jimmy did not seem to react to Leslie they way Joseph and Fred had, so Sara felt a little better about that, and for some reason, Jimmy's presence seemed to put them all at ease. Or maybe it was the fact that Stephanie Trotter accompanied Jimmy. Stephanie was quite an attractive woman herself. She was tall and had long, dark, perfectly straight hair. Stephanie, thought Sara, looked a lot like a young Cher. Take her out of her dark blue business suit and put her into a sequined, low cut gown and she could easily pass for a rock star. The six of them enjoyed a sumptuous dinner, although Leslie and Joseph barely touched their food, another sign of them being in love, thought Sara. During dinner and well into the night, they went over the final plans for the event. Things had come together even better than any of them had anticipated. The guest list included everyone they had wanted there, plus a few surprises. Six senators, including the senior senator from Massachusetts, the Secretary of the Interior, several key figures in the Nevada gaming industry, and some major Las Vegas land developers had not actually been invited, but had called Runningwater to get themselves placed on the guest list. Things were coming together quite nicely and they all knew the event would be a success.

And, as anticipated, it was a huge success. The plan was moving ahead of schedule. Fred had done wonders with investing the money already received before the event, and when the total was announced, pandemonium ensued. It was an amazing ceremony that included Native American drummers and dancers, the highlight of the evening coming when a loin cloth garbed, stunningly handsome youth shot a flaming arrow into the draped wall behind the stage, igniting the drape and sending it into flames, thus revealing a bronze plaque with the name Creation Foundation and the figure $10,000,000,000, the amount that had been committed by the Native American casino owners. The audience went wild. There were tears of joy, whooping and hollering, dancing in the aisles, and a few people, drunk on either the wine or the moment, jumped onto their tables and danced a rather corrupted but enthusiastic version of a Rain Dance, calling on the Great Spirit to rain down more funds into the coffers of the Foundation. By the time Leslie and Sara had made their way to their rooms, the morning sun was rising over the hillside of their eastward facing rooms. They were both exhausted but too excited to sleep and had vowed to meet at 9 a.m. for breakfast.

Chapter 22

Laramie, Wyoming

Tom Barton was eagerly awaiting Leslie's arrival in Laramie so they could put the plan into motion. Sara was coming along with Leslie and although Barton had met Sara only briefly at the Foxwoods event, he was impressed by what he had heard from Leslie and from Runningwater. Brett was in Kansas City on business and would be joining them the following day, as would Fred Simms. They were all still on an emotional high from the Foxwoods event, a state much like what Barton remembered from his college days when he had briefly experimented with drugs. He had never become a serious drug user, partly because he couldn't take the 'downer' that always followed the high, but mostly because he was too much of a control freak to let another person or a drug control his mind and body. It wasn't long after he left college that he discovered he much preferred the high of a successful software product launch or closing a big business deal, to the high he could get from artificial stimulants. And, he had built himself quite an empire in the computer software industry. Of course, there were some 'downers' in business too—a big negotiation gone sour, finding a trusted employee had betrayed him, not having enough time for personal relationships. But the high he was on now was one for which he couldn't imagine a down side. They had laid the groundwork for a major event to launch his project, just as Leslie and Runningwater had planned and successfully completed for the Creation Foundation. And today, they would meet to put the final touches on the plan.

Barton met Sara and Leslie at the airport in his Escalade, throwing their suitcases in the back, after greeting them each with a big hug and kiss. They drove quickly over the windy country roads to the ranch. Leslie had hoped they might have time for a trail ride on his horses again. She felt she had sorely neglected Mancha recently, in fact worried about what would happen to her horses and her ranch with her gone so much. She had brought her riding clothes along just in case. Of course she knew Sara was not big on horses, but she could ride fair enough so she too had packed her jeans although she didn't own cowboy boots. She did throw in a pair of her hiking boots which would surely do should they find themselves meeting on the trail instead of in Barton's office. It turned out that Barton had not planned any riding time. His housekeeper, Consuelo, greeted them at the door, showed Sara and Leslie to their rooms, and assured them she would have coffee and lunch brought into the office because she knew Mr. Tom wanted to get right to work. Well this would be a no-nonsense meeting, thought Leslie; but they did have a lot to do.

During lunch, they reviewed the plan. Leslie was impressed with what Barton and Henderson had already accomplished. The plan was simple but phenomenal. They had obtained permission to hold their event along the fence where years before Matthew Shepard had been brutally murdered. This time, the fence would be used to overcome hatred and violence instead of endorsing it. There were hundreds of people committed to line up along the fence, coupled by chains. Each pair represented a contrast in diversity—a Jew would be chained to a Muslim, a black man to a white man, a gay person to a straight one, an Hispanic to an Anglo, a person with a mental disability to a person with a genius level IQ, a person with a physical disability to a world renowned athlete in prime physical condition, a woman to a man, etc. It was amazing the number of people who had committed to participate in this event—famous athletes, movie icons, artists, and everyday people from every walk of life, all committed to peace and justice. They would form a human fence. Each person would be wearing a specially designed chain bracelet that would be worn going forward as a symbol of breaking down the barriers that separate humankind from itself. Barton had arranged for media from all over the world to cover this event. The computer and entertainment industries would unveil their plans from a huge outdoor stage erected in the field behind the fence. They would preview the new game systems, which would go on sale at midnight that night, on specially built large screens. There would be movie previews of three, new, nonviolent movies endorsing diversity and Barton had signed on several leading rap singers to unveil their new CDs of supporting, uplifting music endorsing diversity and tolerance. He even had managed to recruit a few leaders from the far right and the far left who, although they were the exception rather than the rule, were willing to dialogue with each other in the interests of peace. Leslie could not believe the success he had had. Of course, he had invested a ton of money in this. The highlight of the event would be the official opening of the first Peace and Justice School, which, although it was located in Phoenix, would be unveiled through the magic of multimedia, from the Laramie site.

As in the Foxwoods event, there would also be an unveiling of the amount of money that had been pledged by several big computer companies, software designers and the entertainment and sports industries. As the announcement of the total dollars pledged was made, each couple would break the chains that bound them, join hands and sing, *We Shall Overcome,* with some new verses written especially or the occasion. It was going to be quite an event.

"Wow, is there anything left for us to do?" Sara asked.

"Lots! Let me show you," said Barton, pulling out his laptop computer.

He had the layout of the stage in a special software program that could be zoomed in and out to get intricate views from all angles.

"We need to plan the seating of all the participants, time the presentation, and decide how we're going to symbolize our dollar contributions. I loved the unveiling in Foxwoods, but a flaming arrow won't work here. I am counting on you two to come up with a brilliant idea for that aspect of the event. Tomorrow, when Fred and Brett get here, we need to talk about the details of how we will handle the funding, both income and expenses. Those two guys are the best and Fred's experience with the Creation Foundation should be enough to get Brett started in the right direction to set up our expanded foundation efforts. We're going to have to hire some grant reviewers to help us determine who we will fund and set up some guidelines."

"I agree," Leslie affirmed. "Brett and Fred will be able to lay out a solid plan, I've watched them both in action, especially Fred, and he will be able to get this thing organized in no time. He is bringing a lot of files with him that I am sure we can use; I am not worried about that part at all. But the success of the whole plan hinges on this launch event, so you are right, we need to have it timed down to the second, and the placement of people on the agenda needs to be thought through very carefully. Stephanie Trotter at Foxwoods was a huge help with that. I wonder if we might be able to get her on the phone for a conference call once we've laid out a proposed schedule."

"I can call and get her here by private jet by this afternoon if you think we need her."

Barton was accustomed to getting things done without hesitation and, although he was leader in the technology industry, he had always felt it was best to meet in person when you had something this important to discuss.

"Let's call and see if Runningwater will let us borrow her for an afternoon."

Of course Leslie knew it wasn't quite that simple. Stephanie had a major role at the casino and if they had a big event going on, Joseph might not be too eager to give her up. If she got there this afternoon, they would work well into the night and she would have to come prepared to spend the night. Consuelo, Leslie knew, would not be the slightest bit flustered at another overnight guest, but Stephanie led a pretty well-ordered life and was not accustomed to being whisked off in private planes to travel across the country without at least a few days' notice. Before Leslie had a chance to voice these thoughts, Barton had dialed Runningwater's private cell number from his own cell phone.

"Joe, how is it going? Still raking in all that money?" he laughed.

"Hey, we need Stephanie out her for an afternoon brainstorming session; can I send a plane for her, say in about an hour? I'll have her back by late tonight or if you can spare her for an extra day, she can fly home with Fred tomorrow evening. Tell her, I'll even let her ride my favorite horse."

Leslie felt a little stab of jealousy. How come Stephanie would get to ride? Well, she'd better get to go riding too!

"I guess I'll have to give you all a break now," Barton said to Leslie and Sara, holding his hand over the mouthpiece of the phone.

"Great," he spoke back into the phone. "It will be great to see you both. Call me when you land, and I'll send a car to pick you up. And I'll tell Consuelo to rustle up some more grub for dinner."

Runningwater was coming too, Sara and Leslie realized. This was going to be a long evening!

"Let's get an agenda mapped out and a proposed stage layout, in fact maybe several options, so we can get right to it when Stephanie gets here," suggested Sara.

"I like her style." Barton grinned at Leslie. "I can see why you two have been friends for so long."

Barton secretly wondered if there was ever more to Leslie and Sara's friendship than the platonic relationship they seemed to share, but then Brett always chided him because, as Brett said, Barton thought everyone was gay and he had to stop thinking that there was something wrong with totally straight people. He hadn't been too far off base, at least about Sara. She had occasionally thought about Leslie in a way that was more than friendship, and the fling with Terry, although short-lived, had shown her that making love to a female could be just as fulfilling for her as relationships with men could be, especially since her two marriages had been total failures. In fact, her involvement with the event at Foxwoods had renewed those stirrings in her, as she got to work closely with Stephanie. She almost wished Barton hadn't suggested bringing Stephanie out here, Sara was kind of glad to be out of the way of temptation.

They settled down to work, each of them a bit distracted by their own thoughts of what the night might bring. Leslie wished that Runningwater were not coming, because he always had such a disarming effect on her. Sara was thinking about both Runningwater and Stephanie and was not certain which of them attracted her more. And Barton worried that they wouldn't accomplish all they needed to do today, knowing that Runningwater's main reason for coming along was to see Leslie. But before long, they had several good layouts and a working agenda. They turned next to the question of the climactic moment of the event, the unveiling of the total dollars committed to the Celebrate Diversity Project as they were now calling it, although at this point, they didn't now how much the amount would be.

"How about if each couple brings their chains up to the stage, and as they pile them up, the amount of money can be piling up on a computer screen at the back of the stage," proposed Sara,

"I like that, but it could take a long time," Barton suggested.

"True, but that could help build the suspense, and we could be showing one of the videos or listing the names of the couples on the screen while they're coming forward," offered Leslie.

"Hmm, kind of like beating one's swords into ploughshares," mused Barton.

Leslie was surprised at this Biblical reference; she had not heard Barton quote scripture before. A new idea landed in her head.

"How about instead of just piling up the chains, we have a hot cauldron there, actually melting the chains and at the end, we turn the molten metal into something beautiful?"

Leslie could see it now, although the logistics of it would be difficult to work out.

"It could be done symbolically. The chains are thrown into the 'melting pot' and then poured into a mold, but the finished product would already be produced and it would be taken out of an identical mold and raised for the entire world to see. Now we just need that symbol. What should it be?"

"A ploughshare?" posed Sara. "Whatever the heck a ploughshare actually is!"

"Maybe a bit too obscure," Barton, said, "But good thinking. How about a peace dove? No, that's too trite, and the rainbow is too overused."

Sara and Barton came up with several more ideas, everything from a butterfly to symbolize freedom, to an eagle representing strength. Leslie had been lost in thought and hadn't contributed any ideas until Barton and Sara had just about exhausted every idea they had. All of a sudden, Leslie jumped up out of her chair.

"A Bristlecone Pine tree," she said with a finality in her voice that Sara and Barton were both afraid to question, although they both seemed a bit confused about the idea of how a tree related to what they were doing.

"The oldest living things on earth, a part of creation that existed before any of us were born and will last many years after we're gone. They exist because they have conquered adverse conditions; they grow far enough away from each other so as not to lose their valuable nutrients to another tree and yet close enough so that they can feed off each others' heat and protection. It has to be a bristlecone," Leslie announced.

And so the idea was born. A new logo would be designed for Barton's Foundation and a huge silver medallion would be created, symbolically at least, from the molten chains of slavery, hatred, bigotry, and violence.

After they had finished with their plans, Leslie and Sara sat in the kitchen with Consuelo sipping freshly brewed tea and nibbling on some of Consuelo's famous Mexican cookies while Barton went to the airport to pick up their guests from Connecticut.

Consuelo was preparing dinner, but sat with them for a while, happy to have some female companionship. She was accustomed to a lot of last minute guests at the Barton ranch, the Double B (for Barton and Brett) so she had prepared rooms for Runningwater and Stephanie in no time at all. And she always had plenty of food in the freezer so it wasn't much bother for her to add a few more chickens to the pot and to make a bigger salad.

"You all work too hard," Consuelo sympathized.

"But we love what we're doing; it's so exciting!" Sara countered.

"Well, that is all that matters then. Just like I love to cook, you two love to cook up all those plans and schemes."

Cooking up plans and schemes was what Leslie and Sara were best at. In fact, when they were younger, their friends often referred to them as 'Lucy and Ethel,' and the fact that they were a redhead and a blonde, made this comparison fit them perfectly. Of course they had never before planned anything of this magnitude, and they were certain that Consuelo couldn't begin to know how far-reaching this 'scheme' of theirs would be.

Before long, Barton breezed in the door, looking like the proverbial cat that ate the canary, with Stephanie and Runningwater right behind him. Stephanie looked amazingly refreshed for someone who had just been swept out of her routine and rushed home to pack an overnight bag, before hopping onto a private jet, and flying three-quarters of the way across the country. And Runningwater smiled that beautiful smile of his, before he even saw the three women in the kitchen. The women were all captivated, including Consuelo, who had met Runningwater briefly on his last trip to the Ranch. She thought he looked just like a good Mexican boy, with his dark hair, eyes and skin and those flashing white teeth. She already thought of him as the son she never had and made a big fuss out of getting him a cup of strong coffee and offering to take his bag to his room. Stephanie looked amused at the whole scene. She was accustomed to women falling all over her boss, but she still thought it was interesting that no one seemed to care about her comfort. Sara, sensing what was going on in Stephanie's head, quickly compensated.

"We were just enjoying a cup of tea. Would you like to join us?"

It was a bit of an exaggeration because they had actually finished their tea, but Sara thought Consuelo would step into the role of gracious hostess quickly if she suggested more tea, and she was right. Consuelo went straight to brewing more tea as soon as Joseph had settled into a chair with his coffee.

"Leave the bag. I'll get it later," he said, knowing the effect he had on Consuelo was no different than what he had on most people, men and women alike.

Barton, eager to get right to work, pressed on, "Well, I appreciate you coming all the way out here and I promise you will have time to rest, but I want you to see what we've come up with."

He headed them all in the direction of his office, with Consuelo following closely behind to set up the refreshments. She offered to make a pitcher of Margueritas before dinner, but they all agreed the coffee and tea were fine for now. They knew they had a lot of work ahead of them. Perhaps after dinner they would relax with a drink.

They gathered around the computer screen and reviewed the agendas and the stage set ups. After much discussion, they agreed on the right set up and Stephanie helped them time the script down to the number of seconds it would take people to walk to the podiums. She was an incredible genius at what she did and her sense of timing was amazing. They were all glad she had agreed to come today. She pointed out things that none of them had thought of. By the time they decided it was time to break for dinner, Runningwater had agreed to lend them Stephanie for the week leading up to the event and, of course, the event itself. They were all relieved to know she would be there to hold their feet to the fire and make sure everything went as planned.

There was only one thing they had planned to discuss over dinner and that was the big culmination ceremony. They all decided they could relax after dinner. Barton had promised a surprise for after dinner; he did love his surprises. This time, he assured Leslie, it was smaller than a breadbox. Sara and Stephanie, having no clue what he was talking about threw each other a puzzled look and Stephanie shrugged her firm, square shoulders.

Dinner was delicious and Consuelo bustled around the kitchen bringing all the food in the dining room with that special flair for the dramatic she had. Barton generally ate his meals in the kitchen unless there were guests in the house so the dining room was not well used, but it was comfortable and large enough to seat at least twelve people.

Barton had brought a sketchpad with him along with a notebook, but he had not brought the laptop computer. Runningwater was relieved to see that concession. He much preferred enjoying a relaxing meal and doing business afterward, but he knew Barton wanted to get on to discussing the ceremony, and he could sense the excitement emanating from Leslie, Sara and Barton.

Runningwater and Stephanie loved the plan about melting the chains into the silver medallion and when Runningwater saw the sketch of the Bristlecone medallion Barton had done on the sketchpad, he jumped up out of his seat in amazement. No wonder they were all so excited about this idea. He immediately started to rethink the Creation Foundation logo.

"I have to have that! Let's both use the Bristlecone logo; it fits both our needs. Is that is okay with you?"

He was looking at Barton, but he was certain the idea had come from Leslie and he knew she would agree that he should use it too. Barton deferred to Leslie.

"I am fine with that. It was Leslie's idea, though, so I guess it's up to her."

They all turned to Leslie and she, of course, agreed that they had a common goal, as though there were two different branches of the same tree.

"Of course, it is perfect for both foundations and will send a unified message."

Leslie was already seeing the third branch of her tree taking shape and wondering how the Bristlecone logo would fit into it.

After dinner, they adjourned to the den and Barton pulled out his final surprise and popped it into the DVD player—*Westward the Women*, Leslie's all time favorite movie. She wasn't sure if the rest of them would enjoy it as much as she would, but they all seemed delighted and even Stephanie kicked off her shoes and cuddled up under one of the fleece throws that were on the back of all the chairs and couches in anticipation of cold Wyoming nights. Consuelo arrived with pitchers of Margueritas, and more cookies. The women all shook their heads on the offer of cookies, but Runningwater and Barton dove into them with relish. They were all quiet during the movie and as soon as it ended, Runningwater, Barton and Leslie excused themselves and headed to bed. Sara and Stephanie decided to scan the channels to look for the one that seemed to broadcast *Law and Order* twenty-four hours a day, when they found out they were both 'LAO junkies.'

All except Barton headed out early the next morning to ride the trails. He wanted to finish up his work so he could get to the airport to pick up Fred and Brett. Runningwater and Leslie rode slowly together while Stephanie and Sara urged their horses on to a fast run far ahead of them. As they were riding, Leslie knew it was time she told Runningwater that she was going to be spending some time in Rome with her brother, but she assured him that she would come back for the big Laramie event.

Runningwater had never been out of the United States, nor did he have any desire to do so. He hated flying, but for a minute he was tempted to ask Leslie if he might come to Rome with her and spend some time there. He knew, however, that he couldn't leave the casino staff on its own that long, even with Jimmy and Stephanie at the helm. And, besides, Leslie was being very vague about her business in

Rome, but he got the distinct idea that he wouldn't be welcome. There had always been something about Leslie that he couldn't read, and it was even more apparent on this ride, one that he somehow felt might be their last time alone together. They were riding very close to each other and Leslie reached out and touched his arm as they rode.

"I hope you know how much I care about you, Joseph, and that you also know what a privilege it has been for me to work with you. When I first came to see you, I had no idea if you'd send me packing, thinking I was totally insane. But I knew the minute we met, that this relationship would be a strong one, and one that would bring about some amazing things. Even I couldn't have imagined the depth and breadth of what we've accomplished. And I feel Barton's plan will go just as well. I am so grateful to you for helping out with this project, not to mention all you've done with Creation."

"I too had no idea when we arranged that first meeting what an impact it, and you, would have on my life."

He looked sad for a few minutes, but then he took her hand and stopped his horse under a pinion pine tree. "Will I see you before Laramie?"

"Probably not," she almost whispered, "I will be there a few days before the event though, and I know that Sara and Stephanie have everything under control. Thank you again for letting us 'borrow' Stephanie. I don't know how we would pull this off without her."

"I think she and Sara have found pleasure in each other's company." He tried putting it delicately but he knew what was happening between the two women.

"Yes, I am sure of it." Leslie thought it best to leave it at that.

Leslie and Joseph returned to the ranch long before their two riding partners made their way back. In fact, the two of them had finished breakfast and were in Barton's office when he returned with Fred and Brett. Leslie was pleased to see both men again. She wanted to thank Fred again for everything he had done for the Creation Foundation. And she always enjoyed Brett's company.

Brett came up to Leslie, kissed her on the cheek, and then extended his hand to Runningwater. He was truly glad to see them both. Barton had filled Fred and Brett in on last night's meeting during the drive from the airport. Brett was pleased with the plans, and thought Leslie's Bristlecone logo was fantastic. Fred was a little perturbed that he had already spent money on hiring a graphic designer to create a logo and image for the Creation Foundation, but he knew that Runningwater wouldn't mind the wasted money if he could have the Bristlecone logo that Leslie had come up with and since it was Leslie's creation, he couldn't be too upset about it.

Finally, Stephanie and Sara dashed in looking flushed, and apologized for their tardiness. Stephanie accepted the blame because she loved to ride and knew that Runningwater, at least, would easily believe that she had lost all track of time. He knew she often did that when she was riding back in Connecticut. Sara, on the other hand, was known to not be particularly fond of horses and they both knew that no one would believe that she was so wrapped up in their ride that she forgot about the time. Besides, Stephanie wasn't needed for the financial part of their discussion anyway; this was definitely not her thing. But Sara felt she needed to be in on these discussions since she was helping Fred with the foundation and would likely be working with Brett and Barton on their foundation as well.

The group fished their work that afternoon, and over dinner, Leslie broke the news to all of them that she was going to be spending lot of time in Rome over the next year or two, although she was vague about what she actually was going to be doing there. They, of course, had heard about the Council, mostly from Leslie, since none of them were experts on Church politics and hadn't really followed all the news stories. She explained that she would be helping and advising George on implementing some of the Council's outcomes. She did not mention the Pope at all. Everyone in the group, especially Fred, was a bit mystified by the whole thing. Since when did laywomen advise Cardinals? Of course, none of them was well acquainted with the work of St. Catherine of Siena who advised, and even chided, Popes over five hundred years ago. Fred, a faithful parishioner at St. Thomas, more than any of the others, sensed there was something strange about this whole concept. But he knew enough not to question Leslie.

They had an early dinner and most of the group turned in early as they were all leaving the next morning, each of them with their own thoughts and their own work lying ahead. Leslie and Runningwater were the last to say goodnight, lingering over their after-dinner drinks. Somehow, Runningwater felt like he might be losing his last chance at love, and didn't want to say goodnight at all, but finally Leslie got up, walked slowly across the room, and took Joseph's hand. He stood up and together they walked up the stairs, each to their own room. He wished he had had the nerve to ask her if she would spend the night with him, but he was a proud man and was afraid he would be rejected.

Leslie took the initiative to kiss him goodnight and then, catching him by surprise, leaned very close to his face and slowly and emotionally whispered to him the poem he had given her.

> *"Listen to the air.*
> *You can hear it, feel it,*
> *smell it, taste it.*
> *Woniya Wakan, the holy air,*
> *which renews all by its breath,*
> *Woniya Wakan, spirit, life, breath, river,*
> *it means all that.*
> *We sit together, don't touch,*
> *but something is there,*
> *we feel it between us,*
> *as a presence.*
> *A good way to start thinking about nature,*
> *talk about it.*
> *Rather, talk to it,*
> *talk to the river, to the lakes,*
> *to the winds,*
> *as to our relationship."*

Chapter 23

Rome

And so it began. The longest and most difficult journey of Leslie's life. A journey she had always thought was impossible, and yet, somehow she always knew it was her destiny.

Epilogue

Bethlehem

The morning dawned clear and bright, May 7. As Leslie dressed for Mass that morning, she took more time than usual with her hair and makeup; it had to be just right. Her attire was simple, a plain black, lightweight wool dress, dark hose and pumps, and no jewelry except for a pair of black pearl earrings Michael had bought her on a business trip to China. She was ready five minutes before George pulled up and knocked softly on her door.

"Ready?" he asked, flashing that smile he was so famous for.

The glow on his face and the twinkle in those blue eyes, immediately made Leslie feel at ease. The drive from their hotel to the Church of the Nativity was a short one, but it took forty-five minutes because of the crowds that lined the street. The Pope was here and although the people were not quite sure why or what was happening in the Church of the Nativity, they stood by the roadside, waving and shouting, as the people who greeted Christ with palm branches so many years ago had done.

The location for this liturgical celebration was a choice that surprised even Pope John, but Leslie and George had spent many hours discussing the choice of locations for this momentous occasion and even George was a bit surprised at Leslie's suggestion of the Church of the Nativity over St Peter's Basilica in Rome. While George was anything but traditional, he wondered if his friend, the Pope, would permit such a thing. It certainly broke with all tradition, but, upon reflection, Leslie's idea made a lot of sense to George. After all, this would be a new Nativity, a new beginning for the Church he loved so dearly. The church was surely being reborn. As usual, Leslie won out, and here they were riding to the Church of the Nativity.

The Vatican had alerted the media that the Pope would be celebrating a special Mass in the Church of the Nativity but none of them, not even the Pope's friend and Vatican reporter, Steve Francis, knew exactly what would be happening today. Steve, however, was accustomed to being surprised by this Pope. He had been a reporter for the Vatican for twenty-seven years and had seen three Popes reign. John XXIV was by far his favorite. He was personable and intelligent and besides that, treated the press as though they had intelligence, something the last two Popes never did. To them, the media were a necessary evil, and they tried very hard to depersonalize their relationship with reporters. John XXIV was different from the first day. He invited the media into his office for coffee every Friday and shared his thoughts and his goals with them from the start. He threw open the windows of his office, both literally and figuratively. And, for some reason, he seemed to have a special liking for Steve.

Steve was grateful for their relationship on both a professional and a personal level. He had been a fallen-away Catholic when he was first assigned to the Vatican and he thought his boss must be crazy to expect him to report on the goings on of the Church hierarchy. He slowly began to come back to the Church and shortly after John XXIV took office, Steve asked him to hear his confession, his first in thirty years. While Steve was reluctant to ask a Pope to hear his confession, he felt so close to him from the very first day that he knew if he was ever going to take this step, it had to now and with this Pope. After sharing the sacraments of Reconciliation and Eucharist with the Pope, Steve's respect and admiration for this Pope deepened. And he was thrilled to be invited to travel with the Pope on this trip to Bethlehem. He knew John wanted to tell him what was going on, but the Pope also knew Steve was too good a journalist to not want to scoop his fellow reporters. Steve would be given the full story privately immediately after the Mass was over and that was good enough for him.

Although John XXIV had many detractors among the hierarchy, those who thought he was far too liberal, the common people loved him as no other Pope in recent years. Most of the world's theologians, especially the Americans, supported his decisions to ordain openly gay men, allow priests to marry, reinstate the liberal theologians whom the last Pope had silenced, and other 'radical' changes, although there were still a few who thought he was harming the church by throwing so many of their valued traditions to the wind. George Castle was one of John XXIV's closest friends, a trusted advisor and a staunch supporter of this Pope. Leslie had always been sure that George would be Pope one day if John had anything to do with it. And over the past two years, as she spent so much time with John XXIV, she had sensed this possibility getting closer and closer for George.

George was unusually quiet during the drive to the Church of the Nativity, Leslie thought, but she knew he was probably deep in prayer. This day would surely change his life forever and she knew he would be asking the Holy Spirit for guidance.

Finally, they arrived at the door to the church where it was believed Jesus was born to the Virgin Mary. They were quickly whisked inside the small back room that served as sacristy for the preparation for Mass. Pope John was waiting for them and greeted them both with a kiss on both cheeks. Andre was also there; he would be concelebrating this Mass. Leslie was so proud of Andre, so much like George, and yet so much like Michael. How could one person embody the very best traits of the two men who were such an important part of her life? And, yes, Michael was here too. Leslie never really had understood the meaning of those words which many people utter without thinking, "I'll be with you in Spirit," until now! She knew that Michael was here and his presence was so real, she almost expected to see him standing by her side. Leslie knew that Alex and Valerie would be in the next room rehearsing with the Master of Ceremonies for their part in the celebration. They would be preparing the altar for the consecration of the bread and wine and would be serving at the altar for the liturgy. And her friends Sara, Joseph Runningwater, Tom Barton, Brett Henderson and Fred Simms would be in places of honor in the congregation.

Before long, it was time for everyone to be vested before the liturgy would begin. With all the pomp and circumstance of a Papal Mass, and yet with many new fresh touches that Leslie, George and Pope John XIV had introduced, the time had come at last for the solemn procession down the center aisle of the church. As they processed down the aisle, a million thoughts ran through Leslie's mind all at once. She knew that her family and friends were all there. And most of the College of Cardinals was there to celebrate this historic moment, some reluctantly. A few had refused to attend, begging off sick and some even blatantly defying their Pope with their noticeable absence. Steve Francis, the only representative of the media present, was possibly the only person of those gathered in the Church of the Nativity who was not aware until the entrance procession what was happening. As soon as he saw the entrance procession, Steve understood the significance of what was happening and why his friend the Pope had been so secretive about this day, even with him. Surely, if word had gotten out to anyone except these select people gathered here today, there would have been pandemonium. Even the paparazzi would have ceased their incessant stalking of the rich and famous movie stars to be here today.

Approaching the altar, each of them bowed to kiss it before the liturgy began—George Pope John, Andre and finally the principal celebrant, Leslie! As she began her first Mass, "May God the Creator, the Son and the Holy Spirit be with you," the response resonating in her head, "and also with you," an instant flash back of the past two years came to her. Her intense study with the Pope himself and a few of his trusted Cardinals, her private ordination in the Pope's quarters last evening with only her immediate family present, all that had happened to her in the past few years, and a bit of trepidation about what her life in the future as the first female priest to be officially ordained by the Roman Catholic Church would be like. Leslie knew that although the years ahead would be challenging, men and women all over the world would rejoice in this day. Steve noticed that Pope John XXIV was radiant as she consecrated the Host; perhaps it was his great joy and perhaps even a little bit of pride knowing he would surely be a Pope who would always be remembered for his bringing fresh, new life to the Church, especially because of this day. George gave the most powerful homily Steve had ever heard, speaking about his childhood memories of sister's great faith and her incredible gifts, soon to be shared with so many people. Andre could not have been prouder of his mother. Although he had been shocked when she had first told him she would be studying for the priesthood, he felt there could be no one better suited for the priesthood than Leslie. Valerie and Alex, although they still weren't sure they understood what was happening to their mother and to their Church, knew somehow that through Leslie, many thousands of people's lives would be changed. And Leslie, George and John XXIV knew that each of them had an important role to play in returning the Church to the prophets and the mystics.

Linda Lysakowski, ACFRE

Linda is a well-known author in the non-fiction realm. President/CEO of CAPITAL VENTURE™, a consulting firm for nonprofit organizations, Linda is one of fewer than 100 professionals worldwide to hold the Advanced Certified Fund Raising Executive designation. Linda has trained more than 20,000 professionals in all aspects of development in Canada, Mexico, Egypt and most of the 50 United States.

As a graduate of AFP's Faculty Training Academy, she is a Master Teacher. Linda is the author of *Recruiting and Training Fundraising Volunteers, The Development Plan, Fundraising as a Career: What, Are You Crazy? Capital Campaigns: Everything You Need to Know,* a contributing author to *The Fundraising Feasibility Study—It's Not About the Money,* co-editor of *YOU and Your Nonprofit* and co-author of *The Essential Nonprofit Fundraising Handbook.* She is currently working on *Raise More Money from Your Business Community,* to be published soon.

Linda lives in Las Vegas, NV with her husband, is active in her church and serves as a member of the board of the Women's Ordination Conference.

CPSIA information can be obtained at www.ICGtesting.com
Printed in the USA
244894LV00001B/33/P